Praise for
Lia Matera

"Funny, clear-eyed and strong."

ROBERT B. PARKER

"A right snappy storyteller."

GREGORY MCDONALD

"Di Palma certainly belongs in the same league as Sue Grafton's Kinsey Millhone and Sara Paretsky's V.I. Warshawski when it comes to brains, determination, and guts."

Booklist

THE
SMART
MONEY

Lia Matera

BALLANTINE BOOKS · NEW YORK

ISBN 0-345-37127-5

Manufactured in the United States of America

First Ballantine Books Edition: July 1991

To
Chuck Deininger
and
Dave Woodcock,
wherever you are

1

M<small>Y COUSIN</small> H<small>AL</small> had just moved into a condemned bungalow near the jetty. Everyone else had deserted the development when the foundations cracked and dunes began reclaiming the thoroughfares, so Hal's kerosene lanterns provided the only glimmer of light on the wind-flogged cul-de-sac. He had none of the amenities there—no heat, no water, no company but scrambling sand fleas and other hungry pests. But apparently it suited Hal to keep his staples in glass jars, knowing that rodents and roaches scratched at them like the little match girl at the window.

I stood at the threshold of his hovel. In the lantern light, I could see boarded-up windows, a sand-choked porch, and exterior walls veined with wet cracks. Behind the house, on the opposite shore of the bay, the old nuclear power plant glowed like a neon dinosaur. My hometown.

"Hotshot fucking lawyer." My cousin regarded me with undisguised disgust. "Opening an office in the backwater just so you can stick it to your ex-husband."

"That about sums it up." The wind whipped sand around my ankles, and I could feel my shoulder muscles knot with the cold. "I'm freezing, Hal."

He motioned for me to enter, then preceded me down

a drafty hallway. His sweater was too short and his cor-
duroy pants were threadbare at the seat.

Henry Di Palma, Jr., had once favored button-down
shirts and stiffly pressed jeans. Dozens of them still hung
in the cedar-paneled closets of his father the mayor's house.

In Hal's living room, three lanterns flickered near a
slashed easy chair, and a fire battled the river of cold air
whistling down the fireplace flue. Hal had been sitting
there doing nothing, I guess. There were no books or papers beside the chair, just a jam jar with the dregs of red
wine.

I found a wooden chair and brushed it off, wrinkling
my nose at the dirt that clung to my palm.

"Cleaning lady must have missed a spot," Hal commented.

I sat down and took a good look at him: glowering
brows, deep lines from cheekbone to dimpled chin; eyes
set in a perpetual wince; salt-and-pepper hair that had suffered an impatient and inexpert haircut, self-inflicted.
"Whatever it takes to keep the family away?"

"At least I don't go out of my way to kick them in the
behind."

"Don't waste your sympathy on my ex-husband. He de-
serves it." My high-school sweetheart, Gary Gleason, had
the town's public defender contract. I was going to take it
away from him, and I was going to enjoy doing it. "I'm
just opening up an office. The city doesn't have to accept
my bid."

"Except that you're famous."

"There is that."

A year earlier, I'd defended a man called Wallace Bean,
who'd shot and killed two Republican senators as they stepped
off a chartered jet. I'd managed to assemble that one-in-a-
million jury with enough regard for expert testimony to acquit Bean by reason of insanity. The nation—especially the
conservatives who'd rallied behind the senators' "bombs for

victory" approach to the Vietnam War—had been outraged; but my career had been made. *Time*, *Newsweek*, and other national magazines had carried lengthy articles about the trial—and, inevitably, about me.

"But I'm not exactly popular, Hal."

My hometown was redneck conservative—loggers, fishermen, cannery workers, dairymen; its citizens doubtless disapproved of what the President had called "an abortion of justice." On the other hand, I was a celebrity in a town where people still talked about the time Robert Goulet had stayed overnight at the Hillsdale Inn.

I smiled at my cousin. "All in all, I'd say the smart money's on me."

Hal stroked his jaw—surprisingly clean-shaven—with a long, callused hand. "Well, I happen to like my money the way I like my women: easy."

I glanced around the room. Dust balls scampered across the floor, wood crates did duty as tabletops, broken pieces of furniture glowed in the fire. "I don't see much evidence of either around here."

"No regrets about Bean? Just one more crazy on the street?"

"A medical review board decided my client was sane. *I* didn't make that decision."

"But you represented him—"

"At the sanity hearing? Of course I did. That's my job." The state attorney general had argued against me: *How can a man be crazy in May and sane in April?* And an acerbic psychiatrist had replied, *How can the governor gut the mental health budget and still expect us to provide years of inpatient care?* "It wasn't me who put Bean back on the street."

"So you'll take the credit, but not the blame?"

"Something like that." A damp draft chilled my legs. I tugged the hem of my skirt over my knees. "Why the hermit routine, Hal?"

He smiled, his expression—except for his eyes—suddenly rather sweet. "Didn't the family tell you?"

"You use the war as an excuse to be a self-destructive, ungrateful bum."

"Indulge in an 'I told you so,' if you want." Hal lowered his eyelids, transforming his smile into a smirk.

I'd been vociferously horrified when Hal hadn't resisted the draft—and almost gratified to hear he'd come back from Vietnam moody and waspish. I'd only seen him twice since then. In 1981, I ran into him in Golden Gate Park. He looked haggard and filthy. He told me he hadn't been home in six years. In the winter of 1983, I found him outside my apartment wielding a greasy wrench. He stayed a few days, just long enough to repair his coughing old van. He seemed more relaxed, even amusing in a dry, offhand way. But he wouldn't tell me where he'd been living or what he'd been doing. I didn't mention Hal's visits to our family, as I couldn't say he'd looked a bit prosperous, or even happy. From what I gathered, Hal hadn't contacted them in the two years since. He'd simply appeared at the abandoned development one day last week.

"You know how long the war's been over, Hal? More than ten years." Long enough for me to get divorced; run off to the big city; finish college and law school; clerk for a state supreme court justice; put in a year with the U.S. attorney, criminal division; and join the cream of San Francisco law firms, White, Sayres & Speck. "What's this really about? Why the TV-movie torment?"

"Please. Spare me your philippics."

"And you'll spare me yours?"

Hal laced his fingers behind his head and looked me over. I leaned back in my chair and let him look. My pale olive skin had aged well—no wrinkles at thirty-three—and most men admired my wide-set black eyes and full lips too much to hold my largish nose against me. My belted suit accentuated a small waist, and probably cost more than all Hal's possessions put together. My dainty shoes would cover a month's rent for a three-bedroom house in our mud hole of a town. And my hair, once a wild mass of curls, had been tamed into a damned expensive, side-parted bob. If I didn't look like a competent and very successful lawyer, it wasn't my fault.

"I liked you better when you looked like Mowgli," was my cousin's verdict.

"You're behind the times, Hal. This is how we dress in the jungle nowadays."

"So why come back here? You always hated the rain."

"You just told me. To stick it to my ex-husband."

He shook his head. "So you get the goddamned public defender's contract, and Gleason scrambles a little. He'll get by; he always has."

"Don't bet on it!" I was surprised to hear the venom in my tone; I've had a lot of practice keeping anger out of my voice ("With all due respect, Your Honor . . ."). I changed the subject. "Are you coming to my office-warming party?"

"My parents going to be there?"

"What do you think?" Not a word from them in the years they'd considered me "loose" for running off to San Francisco, but they'd been in the aisles with their cameras when I graduated from law school.

"I think I have a previous engagement." The firelight accentuated the harsh creases in Hal's cheeks.

"And I think you've worn out the war as an excuse."

"Any suggestions for a better one?"

I indicated his surroundings. "Shame that your daddy rammed this boondoggle down the planning commission's throat."

He sat up abruptly. "Laura, my dear, you should be grateful to my daddy the mayor. He had to put your ex-husband in the hospital to build this little bit of hell."

"Every cloud has its silver lining, Hal."

Hal rested his forearms on his knees. "What did Gleason do to you, anyway?"

"It's something he's going to do *for* me." There was still a whisper of wrath in my voice, but only a whisper. "Once he sees that nothing else will get me out of town."

Fire shadows capered over the bare walls and cobwebbed ceiling. Hal's voice was unusually quiet. "Gleason coming to your office-warming?"

"I'd say so. He wouldn't want to appear ungracious."

"So you did invite him."

"Why, Hal! There's no one I'd rather see there."

2

I HUNG MY jacket in the hall closet and tried to stifle that buried-alive feeling I always get when I see the gilt rococo mirrors and satin floral settees that are fixtures in the mansion my father shares with Hal's parents. My father has been a widower for thirty years, but he and I and a housekeeper always lived in the house my mother had chosen for us. It wasn't until I got married that my father sold the brick bungalow and moved in with his second cousin, my "Uncle" Henry.

I found Papa in his study, feet, in gleaming black shoes, crossed on top of his account books. His black hair was sleekly combed and his jowly face dignified as he stared out the window, smoking a tiny cigar. He was a short, powerful man, with a large pug nose, a firm, fleshy face, and cunning, short-lashed eyes.

"I've been to see Hal," I told him.

He dropped his feet to the floor. " 'Hal'! My cousin's name isn't good enough for his son?"

"Henry, then." I didn't feel like fighting the battle of the name for Hal again. At age sixteen my cousin had begun to insist his contemporaries call him Hal. (Years later, I read *Henry IV, Part I,* and finally got the joke.) He also refused to touch his birthday present—a brand-new Fiat Spider I'd have killed for.

Papa shook his head and muttered, "He lives in a slum when he could live in a palace!"

A slight exaggeration. The ":Mayor's Residence" (easy to think of it as my Uncle Henry's own house, since he'd been mayor for twenty-seven years) was a ten-bedroom mock Swiss chalet, ludicrously out of keeping with the town's bungalows and Victorians. But it was certainly no palace, in spite of having been pretentiously overdecorated at the taxpayers' expense.

"I don't think Aunt Diana appreciates his, um, rough charm." The understatement of the year. Hal's mother had nothing but disdain for those less shallow, wealthy, and insincere than herself. The town Babbitts appreciated her unbridled ambition and ostentatious display of wealth; but those attributes weren't particularly desirable in a mother, not if you happened to be an antisocial pauper like Hal.

"Anyway, Hal—Henry—is too old to live at home."

Papa stubbed out his cigar, brushing ashes off his vest. "He's too old to live like a gypsy, you mean."

"I rented a house today."

Papa's nostrils flared but he said nothing; a victory for me that he considered it useless to remonstrate. We both knew my Aunt Diana would speculate that I lived alone to entertain men, a proposition that would be unbearable to my papa if I lived to be a hundred. He was still struggling to accept my divorce. He told me at the time—told me until I stormed out of town—that boys will be boys, and a wife should understand the ways of the world.

"A Victorian on Clarke," I continued.

Papa was startled; I carefully checked my smile. That three-block strip of Victorians had been restored to look like fern bars, with oak floors and beveled windows. It was as pricey as the town got, and it was where my ex-husband kept house with his girlfriend, Kirsten Strindberg. In fact, my new house, a drafty six-bedroom, was directly across the street from my ex-husband's.

My Aunt Diana stepped into the room. She was a tall woman with high, arched brows, a long, thin nose, and a tiny chin she tucked down into a plump neck. She greeted me with cold cordiality. That morning she'd suggested that I let her and my uncle host my office-warming party. ("It doesn't look *good* for a young girl to put herself forward.") My snub had, of necessity, been forceful, and Aunt Diana had decided to punish me by remembering "other plans."

"Shall I have them set a place for you at dinner?" my aunt inquired.

"I have to be somewhere at seven," I lied. "Sorry."

"Dieting?" She sniffed, regarding my trim figure. "They say that after thirty a woman has to choose between her face and her figure."

Equally daunting options, in my aunt's case.

I spent most of the evening driving around town. For fourteen years, I'd associated Hillsdale with feeling trapped, understimulated, suffocated by my family, and—worst of all—shamed by my husband. Now I drove the streets and found that the place hardly even looked familiar. It was just a sprawling Pacific Northwest town smothered in gray drizzle, with big square houses on big square lots, wide streets with high curbs and huge storm drains, a lot of muddy hills and gullies, and a fishy smell from the redeveloped marina. The occasional metal hitching post could still be seen poking through a damp sidewalk, and the flophouses near the boat basin had been repainted and marked with historical plaques. After the cramped bustle of San Francisco, there was something rather grand about the well-tended old neighborhoods, with their dripping rhododendrons and giant rose bushes. I remembered the five-foot skunk cabbages in the gully behind my old house; I hadn't thought of them in years.

I parked my car in front of the house I'd just rented. I turned up the heater and stared at the house across the street. My ex-husband's house was a two-story Victorian with a domed roof. It looked cared for, painted tan with rust-and-navy trim. A green Peugeot was cozily tucked into the gingerbread carport. Red and purple rhododendrons were in flower, the lawn was neat, the porch was hung with huge planters of fuchsia.

I wondered where Lennart Strindberg was buried, whether his grave was as manicured as my ex-husband's lawn. But Kirsten probably preferred to tend to the living.

The living. I supposed my plan was clever; it was the best I could do under the circumstances. But it was only a half measure. It wasn't a bomb; it wasn't a knife in the ribs.

I remembered Kirsten's nasty little habit of getting Lennart to fetch and carry for her, of making her round little doll's face look plaintive as she said, "Len, more coffee for everyone?" or "Len, could you get the groceries?"

Lennart Strindberg, six feet four, translucent white skin over pronounced cheekbones and a delicate nose, hair the color and consistency of corn silk, long-fingered hands, faraway gray eyes, and an unhappy set to his too-wide mouth: Lennart Strindberg was the handsomest man in the world, I had thought.

And he'd fetched and carried for Kirsten, quietly, so quietly. I'd never seen him pause or hesitate. "No" had not been in his lexicon.

Kirsten used to chide me in Gary's presence. "You spoil Gary!" she'd exclaim coyly when she learned I'd done some simple thing for him. Then she'd narrow her eyes and add, "*I*'d beat him into shape fast enough." And Gary would respond with an "Oh, would you?" grin.

Lennart Strindberg told me, the very last time I saw him, that Kirsten hated to be obeyed, that it made her feel unwomanly.

"Then why do you do it?"

Lennart had shrugged. "Good manners are most necessary when they are not appreciated."

Lennart Strindberg. All these years I'd thought of him as a living, breathing human being. All these years I'd wondered if we'd ever meet again, if he'd ever change his mind about me—"wise up," as it were.

And all these years, Lennart Strindberg had been dead.

Dead so long that Kirsten and Gary probably thought of him only rarely, thought of him with little guilt and less remorse.

But I would change that. Indeed I would.

3

THE OFFICE-WARMING WAS going well.

I'd bought a great deal of expensive champagne, and I was doing my best to charm magistrates and judges—the ones who informally advised the county whom to select for public defender.

I let my Uncle Henry lead me around the room, introducing me to people I already knew. Uncle Henry was short and barrel-chested, like my father, with the same dark, firm skin and sleek black hair. But my Uncle Henry wore an expression of false candor, of goodwill, that my father could never, nor would ever need to, feign.

Uncle Henry was in a good mood that afternoon, slapping backs and telling jokes that would have made my Aunt Diana tight-lipped with disapproval.

I was standing with our congressman, a bloated bald man with a squashed strawberry of a nose. I was defending—for the thousandth time—"TV syndrome," a phrase I'd coined during Wallace Bean's trial. Bean had been hooked on the type of television fare that glamorized violence and intrigue, that showed one brave man breaking the rules, beating the system, changing history. When he stepped in front of the airplane steps with his forty-five, Bean saw himself as the savior of liberalism, the avenger of dead draftees, the man who would purge America's psyche of an unjust war.

Bean's jury hadn't based its insanity verdict on the TV-syndrome defense, though. It had been a fallback argument: Even if Bean *was* insane, I'd asserted, he'd been too confused by television violence-for-a-good-cause to realize that his actions were antisocial or wrong.

Unfortunately, the press—and even many lawyers, who should have known better—thought Bean had been acquitted because he'd watched too much television. TV syndrome had become a catchphrase for the subversion of justice by sneaky defense lawyers. In the year since the trial, I'd been on a dozen talk shows and given a hundred newspaper and magazine interviews to clear up the misconception, but people seemed determined to believe in the perversity of the legal system.

I was tired of trying to set the record straight. To the fat congressman, I said merely, "Bean's was the first generation to base its concept of reality on what it saw on network television, sir. That's rather frightening, when you think about it."

I'd heard the congressman's rejoinder so many times— *we all watch TV, but we don't all kill senators*—that I put my brain on hold and began discreetly scanning the room, looking for an excuse to slip away.

And I saw Gary Gleason, standing near the door.

He wore a shiny sharkskin suit that looked straight out of a parcel with a Tokyo postmark. The bastard had kept slim, though; he'd aged well. He was shorter than I remembered, long in the torso and short-legged. His hair had thinned from an unmanageable tangle of brown frizz to a shorter, wispier style that showed more forehead than it had in his youth. And his face—well, it was similar enough to the face I had fallen in love with to make me recall some of the old feeling. Some, but not much.

It still wore a habitual, thoughtful frown; his hazel eyes

still peered out from the shade of it. His nose was straight, short and perfect. He still wore a full mustache on his long upper lip, though he'd shaved the bushy sideburns.

But he looked older. His cheeks were less plump, and there were squint lines around his eyes and frown lines in his forehead. And there was an aura of wariness about him—natural under the circumstances, perhaps—that was unlike the cocky arrogance of his youth.

My ex-husband, unaware of my scrutiny, looked around my well-appointed offices, shaking his head slightly.

I excused myself and strode toward him. Out of the corner of my eye, I saw my papa watching, saw him grow still and tense, his hand poised in midair with his cigarette lighter aflame, like a torch.

Gary became aware that I approached, looked me up and down, forgot to smile.

"It's been too long," I lied. I shook the once-familiar hand and thought, *You bastard, just wait*. "How's your practice going?"

He dropped my hand quickly. "Fine—great. Too great, really. There's plenty of work in this town for a few more lawyers." He glanced at the four rooms that composed my office suite.

"It's just me," I told him. "I'll be in that office." I pointed to one with a view of the courthouse. "I'll install a detective in the one at the end, and the computer system in the one next to me. And the receptionist out here, of course."

He glanced out the nearest window to hide his surprise; I remembered that mannerism. The window framed the main street of downtown, which was also part of Highway 101. A fifty-foot logging truck rattled by, a pyramid of redwood logs strapped to its trailer. For a moment, it obscured my view of Woolworth's.

"Your own detective, huh?"

I nodded. "I like to have my own; I like the convenience. And I've gotten very high-tech lately. How about you? Have you entered the computer age?''

He shook his head. "We're still using typewriters. In fact, you might have trouble finding a qualified secretary up here if your system's very sophisticated.''

"I'll be using one of White, Sayres & Speck's paralegals for a while, while the firm moves to new offices. A real computer whiz, she is.'' I smiled. "I think she agreed to come because of Sandy, my detective; he looks a lot like Gary Cooper.''

A slight rigidity of the chin told me Gary was bothered. "That's great.''

"How's Kirsten?'' I hated speaking her name.

He met my eye. "Fine.''

"Any kids?''

Kids were a complication for which my plan made no allowance. I was relieved to hear Gary say, "No. Not yet.''

Time for the opening salvo: "I found out recently that Kirsten is White, Sayres & Speck's landlord.''

Gary looked startled. A slight flush started up his neck. He didn't say anything.

"In fact, she's the reason the firm's moving. Their lease expired, and the rent's going up almost a thousand percent.''

Gary frowned. "I guess the only businesses in San Francisco getting bargains on rent anymore are the ones with the fifteen- and twenty-year-old leases.''

"Not like here,'' I agreed. "When I heard how low the rent was on this office, I couldn't believe it.'' I waited until Gary began to look comfortable again. "But maybe now that Kirsten will be getting fair market value on those San Francisco offices, you'll be able to invest in some computers.''

Gary squinted at me, preparing a reply.

I added casually, "By the way, did you know we're neighbors?"

"Neighbors?" He looked horrified.

"My father says you live on Clarke Street. I just rented a house there myself. Number One Fifty-seven."

"What are you—?" For a moment I thought Gary would lower the facade. But he caught himself, burying his fists in his pockets and observing, "We're right across the street."

"Tell me, do you ever seen Lennart Strindberg?" I noticed how quickly his flush died into pallor. "It's been what, fourteen years since I last saw him. I thought I'd give him a call if he's still in—"

"He died." Gary's tone was cautious. He didn't believe that I didn't know.

I didn't care what he believed. "Lennart *died*?"

"Several years ago." Fourteen years ago. "I'd have let you know—I assumed you did know." He continued to watch me, uncertain now.

"And who did you think would tell me?" I let him see a little of the anger I felt.

Gary looked away. "I thought your father—I'm sorry."

"Are you?"

We made eye contact again; I'd startled him all right.

"Yes, I am," he murmured.

"Then perhaps you'll stop by my house later and tell me what happened."

He frowned, hesitating.

"This isn't the place to discuss it," I pointed out.

The frown deepened. "All right."

"Seven o'clock?"

He nodded.

I turned to greet another guest before Gary could see my smile. But my papa, his lighter burnt out and lowered, did see it.

What he made of it, I don't know.

4

THE RECEPTION BROKE up at five o'clock, leaving me a little high on champagne, and too restless to go home with my papa and my uncle.

I grabbed a couple of bottles of champagne and sped to Hal's. I had a fancy to get him drunk and make him laugh.

I managed neither. My cousin didn't invite me into his collapsing bower. Instead, he took the champagne bottles and started walking, apparently expecting me to follow. I picked my way over buckled sidewalks strewn with warped window frames and sandy strips of carpet. On either side of us, two-story houses rose from a litter of broken glass, dune weeds, and beer cans. Doors were nailed shut, windows were boarded up, and tattered condemnation notices flapped in the salty wind. Here and there, doors had been pried open, revealing carpetless floors, bits of abandoned furniture, and appliance-looted kitchens. Walls were graffittied with parodies of the developers' motto, ''Luxury You Can Afford.''

Then, fighting a freezing blast of wind, we crossed the sand flats that separated the sinking development from the bay. Hal led me to a jetty of giant, jagged rocks extending like a crooked finger out to sea.

I turned up my jacket collar. It was always painfully, miserably cold out on the jetty, and that evening was no exception. Waves battered the saw-tooth granite and the wind whistled with sprays of spindrift.

"Not worried about your fancy clothes?" Hal inquired sardonically.

"I've got others," I assured him.

He popped both champagne corks and handed me one of the bottles, sucking froth from the other. "Expensive taste in liquor."

"In everything."

"Things." He sat beside me on a narrow ledge of rock. "They that important to you?"

"Things, no. Appearances, yes. They're my stock-in-trade, Hal. My clothes, my car, my things tell the men around me—and it's the only way to make some of them listen, believe me—that I have power, that I have brains, that I have ability."

"Bullshit. It tells them you have money."

"Try the champagne. You'll be glad I have money."

Hal drank. A third of the bottle, almost. A seasoned drinker, it seemed.

The jetty ended where the bay met open sea. From where I sat, I could see the bay curve past Hillsdale's corrugated fish canneries and oyster farms, past the dock-side Victorians of its first timber magnates. Across the bay, behind a bare strip of muddy sand, a nuclear power plant rose in an intricate pattern of white lights and metal braces. It was one of the first things my Uncle Henry had acquired for the town when he'd become its mayor. The plant was obsolete and out of commission now, a potential catastrophe for the next hundred and fifty thousand years.

"What are you after, Laura dear?" Hal set the bottle between his knees, both hands still around its neck. "What are you getting me drunk for?"

"Your body?"

"No." My cousin didn't flatter easily. "You go for the body beautifuls. Part of your class act. The sports car, the clothes—and the hunk in the five-hundred-dollar suit.'' His eyes had begun to glaze, just a bit.

I looked him over: broad shoulders, big arms, slender hips. An Yves Saint Laurent would work.

''The last man I was in love with didn't even own a suit, Hal. He was very unpretentious and quiet, but you could tell by his eyes that he had a soul, you know what I mean?''

Hal looked down at his bottle, running his finger along the wet lip to make it hum. ''So what became of your soul-eyed love? You get some clever revenge on him, too, like you're going to get on your ex-husband?''

''He's dead.''

Hal smiled down at me. He looked misleadingly sweet. ''Happens to a lot of nice people, Mowgli.''

I was more than a little tipsy, staring up at him.

He slid away to the farthest corner of the ledge. ''Don't look at me like that.''

''Like what?''

''Like I'm a pair of shoes in a shop window.'' He shook his head. ''I am *not*, I repeat *not*, for sale.''

''Meaning, I'm not your type? I already know that. You like your women the way you like your money. Borrowed without interest, quickly spent. Dumb as hell.''

''Oh, I'll fuck a smart one.'' His grin was ironic. ''If she's determined to slum it. But never a heartless one, never a Snow Queen like you.''

If he thought he could hurt my tender feelings by insulting me, then he didn't know many litigators.

I poured out the rest of the champagne, watching it make a fizzy puddle in a crevice of rock. ''Men like to believe successful women are unwomanly, Hal. They like to think we couldn't have made it without being bitches.''

I glanced at him. His expression was misogynistic. I added, ''Whoever got her hooks into you did a great job.

If I'd done a tenth as much damage to Gary, I'd be satisfied."

I handed him the empty bottle. "Here. Recycle it. And maybe someday you'll be able to afford another."

I walked away, staggering into a wall of wind. Before I'd gone twenty paces, I heard the champagne bottle shatter on the rocks.

5

I TOOK THE long way home, winding through the renovated waterfront. What had once been an honest slum of warehouses, thrift shops, and bars now had a brand-new "olde" look. A fountain, a statue, new cobblestones, and fresh paint embellished some modest art galleries, "taverns," and import stores. But there wasn't a tourist in sight. It would take more than a touch of Disneyland to draw people to a rainy town three hundred miles from the nearest city; it would take more than a few oyster bars to revive an economy that had clear-cut its way out of the timber business and fished its bay to depletion. It amazed me that term after term, bad idea after bad idea, the township of Hillsdale kept reelecting my Uncle Henry to solve its problems.

It was starting to get dark when I turned onto Clarke Street. The clock on my dashboard said six-fifty, and it was always right. I'd barely have time to de-Mowglify my hair before Gary Gleason arrived at seven. I was hoping the movers had unpacked all my toiletries, when I noticed the commotion on my block.

Two police cars, an ambulance, and a car from a nearby fire station—all with red lights flashing—blocked the street in front of my house. Onlookers huddled in hushed groups, looking somber in the twilight. Men in white uniforms knelt in the middle of the street. Fire fighters stood directly behind them. Policemen urged bystanders to go back to their houses.

One policeman stood behind a tall woman in a Mexican peasant dress. His hands were on her shoulders, and he was forcing her back, away from whatever lay in the road.

I parked my car and approached the crowd. I was just about to ask someone what had happened, when I got a closer look at the woman in the peasant dress. It was Kirsten Strindberg.

She was more beautiful than I remembered, with a heart-shaped face, wide-set blue eyes, and a peachy, unblemished complexion. Her hair was pale gold, blunt cut to her shoulders, with full bangs. Her figure was hidden in the loose folds of her peasant dress, but I supposed (bitterly) that it was still terrific.

At this moment, her lips were pulled back with anxiety, her eyes were puffy and streaming tears, and her hair looked as though she'd been dragging her fingers through it.

Something terrible had happened to Gary Gleason; nothing else would account for the tableau.

I pushed past the spectators, knocking aside a policeman's arm. I elbowed my way between two fire fighters who stood behind the kneeling paramedics.

Lying crumpled in the roadway, while a paramedic gingerly examined his abdomen, was my ex-husband, a few streaks of dirt on his face, his eyelids fluttering.

"Gary! What happened?"

One of the fire fighters snapped, "Christ!" and tried to nudge me back behind him. He reeked of English Leather.

I distracted him with an elbow to the rib cage. I repeated, "What happened?"

Gary Gleason's eyes fluttered open for a moment. "Kirsten?"

"Laura."

He looked up at me, wincing. He murmured, "It was Franco," then he closed his eyes again, shuddering.

The paramedic barked, "Get her out of here!"

A cop materialized behind me, grabbing my arm and pulling me back.

English Leather said, "He told her something."

I glanced at the cop. He was a young man with a wall of stupidity behind his eyes.

"Yeah?" The cop tried to look hard-boiled. "What was it?"

"I didn't hear," I lied.

The cop's grip tightened on my arm. He turned to English Leather and repeated the question.

"Dunno." The fire fighter pulled off his cap and wiped his forehead with his wrist. "Sounded like, 'It was fun to go,' or something like that."

"He came to a party at my office today; he must have meant that." I jerked my arm free. "Was this a hit-and-run?"

The young cop nodded sourly. "Who are you? Family?"

"Neighbor."

"Well, go home. Everything's under control."

The paramedics lifted Gary onto a stretcher.

English Leather muttered, "How many points for running over a lawyer?" and his partner snickered.

Kirsten, glancing at me with shocked eyes, followed the stretcher into the ambulance.

The ambulance pulled out, siren screaming, followed

by the fire car and one of the two police cars. The other squad car continued to block the street, its radio squawking.

I stood there for a while, staring at my ex-husband's house. The curtains were drawn and the lights were on. The front door was open, just a crack.

I thought about what Gary Gleason had said to me. It seemed—and it had to be—impossible.

I went inside my house. The movers had put things pretty much where I wanted them, and the result was pleasing, if unlived-in. I'd leased most of the furniture from an antique dealer, and the gleaming old pieces looked good in the small Victorian rooms.

I wandered through the house, missing my own less elegant things, wishing myself back home in San Francisco.

Six months. In six months I'd be home. White, Sayres & Speck wouldn't put up with a longer absence. It had been good publicity for them, my winning the Bean case; they would humor me—for a while. But my savings account wouldn't last much longer than six months—not the way I was throwing cash around.

In five months, Hillsdale's board of supervisors would award the public defender contract. I'd planned to establish myself quickly, win the contract away from Gary Gleason, then strike my bargain with him. Once Gary accepted my terms and conditions, I would decline the contract, and go home.

But if Gary did not recover soon, or did not recover fully . . . There was nothing to be gained by sticking around defending rednecks who'd had a few too many. No, if Gary was seriously hurt, I was through.

Damn him! Not only had he put my inconvenient and expensive plan in jeopardy, but he'd added an additional complication.

I had to make sure he didn't repeat to the police what he'd just said to me.

It couldn't be true, for one thing. Daylight had been waning. Gary had certainly been mistaken. Or he'd been lying.

Because my papa, Franco Di Palma, would *not* have run from the scene of an accident.

6

AFTER I'D SHOWERED and changed my clothes, I telephoned the hospital. A southern-accented voice told me Gary was in "stable condition," whatever that meant. The woman wouldn't elaborate.

I parted my front curtain and stared at my ex-husband's house, thinking about the year and a half we'd been married: Dropping mescaline in a room with red light bulbs; discussing J. D. Salinger and listening to Leon Russell; going to sleazy dockside bars to prove we'd severed our middle-class roots; opening a "Peace Center" and running off "Peace Letters" on an ancient Gestetner; George Carlin records, Firesign Theater; a group of us skinny-dipping and nearly freezing in Jay Bartoli's parents' pool (not a trace of suntan on our goosefleshed bodies); Bartoli propositioning me in the water, showing off his muscles. But Gary had been the smarter man; that was all that mattered to me.

They'd known about Gary and Kirsten, all our Peace Center friends; I'd run away because I couldn't face them.

I closed the musty curtain, flowered damask that had hung here for thirty years, perhaps, with little bright sun to fade it. I had seen what I wanted to see: Gary Gleason's front door was still slightly ajar.

I'd have been a fool to pass up an opportunity like that.

I waited until the squad cars had driven off and the last of the neighbors had gone home. When I was reasonably sure no one was watching, I slipped across the street. I could always say I'd noticed the open door and come like a good neighbor to close it.

But no one spotted me. I went inside unimpeded.

My ex-husband's furnishings were much like his clothes, serviceable but not stylish. His couches and chairs were mismatched, showing signs of wear. There were books and plants in every nook and on every shelf. The place was reasonably tidy, but it had been a while since anyone had vacuumed the rag rugs or dusted the top of the grandfather clock.

I didn't know what I was looking for, really. Some memory of Lennart, I guess. If his ghost were anywhere, it would be with the woman who'd lied to him for months while she'd carried on her affair with my husband.

I glanced into all the downstairs rooms. The kitchen table was set and a casserole baked in the oven, the timer showing a few minutes left on the cycle. A half-finished square of needlepoint was on the floor near the back door, threads and needle dangling.

I peeked out at the back porch. The daisy-ringed yard was pleasant but unkempt. A broken clay planter rested on the steep stairs, an azalea beginning to droop in its loose dirt. An empty macramé plant hanger swung from a nail below the rain gutter, a foot-long two-by-two caught in its mesh, thumping against the porch supports.

Upstairs, in the bottom drawer of Kirsten's vanity, I

found something worth taking. It was a bundle of old letters. A few of them were in Lennart's handwriting, but most were from Gary. I considered leaving those behind, but decided to take all of them.

I read them at home that night, with a bottle of vodka beside me. I needed it, too, to control my disgust. Men were such fools, such asses.

7

I SLID INTO the parking place in front of my papa's brontosaurus-sized Lincoln. The black car appeared gray in the fog-dimmed glow of the streetlight across the street.

There were no lights on in the mayor's "chalet." My dashboard clock read 11:48; I'd been drinking for a good long while, reading Kirsten's goddamned letters.

I cut my lights, and climbed out of the car. It was hard to see the Lincoln's front bumper in the dim light. It wasn't mashed, that much was apparent. But a massive car like that wouldn't show much damage if it broadsided a moose.

I pulled a towel out of my car. With it, I wiped down most of the Lincoln's front end. It's usually blood and fibers that convict hit-and-run drivers.

Then I groped in the misty darkness, feeling for crumpled metal. I found a few snails gliding along the bumper on a film of dew. And I also found a rough spot. It was slight, just some scratches and depressions near the headlight on the driver's side, nothing to notify the insurance company about. It probably meant my papa had pulled too far forward trying to maneuver out of a tight parking spot.

But I climbed back into my convertible—a Mercedes 380SL I'd waited six weeks for—drove forward twenty-five feet, shifted into reverse, and rammed the Lincoln at about twenty miles per hour.

It was downright painful hearing metal meet metal. The chances of finding a new back bumper for a 380SL here in the outback were slim. But that's what it was all about; my rear bumper and my papa's front bumper had to be a matched set.

In the morning, I'd call and apoligize, tell my papa I'd come for a late visit, crumpled his bumper, and gone home, seeing that the house lights were off.

If he sounded furious with me, I'd be relieved. If he sounded relieved, I didn't know what the hell I'd do.

I was about to pull away and go home, when a gray shape squatted beside my door, tapping on my window. I nearly screamed.

Then I recognized the outline of the rude haircut. I hit the button to lower the window.

"Some very poor driving, there, Mowgli," my cousin Hal commented.

"Don't scare me like that," I complained. "And I don't need a running commentary on the state of my hair!"

He chuckled. "I'd hate to see you try to pass a field sobriety test right now, Mow—Laura."

"I'm very coordinated when I'm drunk, Hal."

"I used to think I was too. Till I ended up spending a month in the slammer."

"Did you really? Where?"

"Massachusetts. Here," he opened the car door. "Move over. I'll drive. If I can untangle these bumpers."

I considered protesting, then slid over.

Hal eased away from my papa's Lincoln, listening for falling parts. "You want to leave him a note?"

I shook my head. "I'll call him in the morning."

"You usually visit him at midnight, Mowgli?"

"Do you, Hal?"

Hal fiddled with the stick shift for a moment, and I thought of Lennart, who'd been too inept to work the gears of my old VW bug.

He pulled away from the curb, remarking, "Nice car. Better than you deserve, if this is typical of your driving."

"What are you doing here, anyway? How'd you get here?" His van was history.

"Walked."

"Walked? It must be ten miles."

"So, you think your papa tried to run down Gary Gleason?" Hal's face was saturnine in the pale green glow of dashboard lights. "That's why you rammed his bumper, isn't it?"

"How did you know Gary got hurt?"

"Heard it on the news."

"You don't have electricity."

"I do have a transistor radio."

"So you hiked ten miles into town to skulk around your father's house?"

He leaned back in the seat, driving in silent enjoyment for a moment. "I hiked in to get to a phone. The hospital says Gleason's okay." He smiled mirthlessly. "But I suppose you've been phoning every ten minutes—"

"And pacing the floor with anxiety. Naturally. What were you doing at your father's house?"

"Looking for you."

"What did you want me for?"

"Just thought I'd comfort you in your hour of distress. You know, you smell like Saturday night at the drunk tank. That's interesting."

"I'm interesting much of the time, Hal."

We stopped at a light, and Hal turned to consider me. I'm not sure what he made of me; the light changed.

When we got to my place, Hal followed me inside.

He settled himself on my rented camelback couch, and I went upstairs to wash and try to sober up a bit.

When I came back downstairs, I found him seated at my desk, nursing a glass—my glass—of vodka. In his other hand he held one of Kirsten's letters from Lennart. The expression on his face was arrestingly bitter.

I strode across the room and snatched the letter away. "Damn you, Hal!"

"Love letters? Awfully sentimental of you, Mowgli."

I frowned at Lennart's cramped handwriting. The words, *I love you dearly—please don't do this to me*, leapt to the eye.

"Sentimental? I guess so. I broke enough laws to get them. Look, just forget you saw them here, will you?"

Hal gazed at my stack of borrowed letters. "Broke enough laws," he repeated thoughtfully. He handed me the glass of vodka. "Tell me about the guy with the soul in his eyes. And I'll forget I saw the letters." There was a flicker of irony in his smile.

"Give me a break, Hal. What do you care?"

"The whole family's out to get Gary Gleason all of a sudden. I want to know why. And this soul-eyed guy, he's got something to do with it."

"No one's 'out to get' Gary but me."

"Gleason's been in the hospital twice in the last few years. The first time, my father put him there."

"Indirectly. Very indirectly." Gary had organized a sit-in to block construction of the development that now housed Hal and his cockroaches. The "luxury subdivision" paved over wetlands where egrets bred, and Gary, it seemed, was a great conservationist. Not so my Uncle Henry. Loyal to his land-developer friends, he'd asked the police captain to have the demonstrators removed by force.

And in Gary's case, the force had been predictably excessive; cops don't like public defenders.

Hal continued, "And now you're smashing up your car so no one will be able to say your father ran Gary down."

"He didn't! I didn't! I just—"

Hal picked up a couple of Kirsten's letters. "I know someone who'd love to know you've got these, Laura."

I crossed the room and sank into the couch, swallowing what remained of my vodka. "Christ, I wonder how many people get blackmailed by their own relatives."

"Why not? Why not blackmail? Look at our goddamned family, and tell me where you'll find more greed, more vanity, more acquisitiveness." Hal ran his fingers through his hair. "So tell me about Soul-eyes."

I told him.

8

"THAT'S THE STORY?" Hal sounded disappointed. "You try for months to get this Strindberg guy to cheat on his wife, and the whole time she's laying your husband?"

"I'm sorry it's not more titillating."

"So what did Soul-eyes do when he found out about his old lady and Gleason?"

"Came to me."

"And?"

"What do you think?"

"I think you should have let him hang on to his moral superiority."

"I was in love with him!"

Hal shook his head. "No, you weren't."

"What do you know?" Admittedly a lame retort, but I'd had a couple more shots of vodka.

"Not very damned much. You still haven't told me how Soul-eyes died, and why everyone in the family is going after Gary Gleason a decade later."

An obnoxious buzzing filled the room.

Hal looked peeved. "Saved by the bell. You expecting company?"

"At two in the morning? What do you think?" I parted the curtain behind my couch and strained till I could see my front porch. "It's Kirsten!" I looked at Hal, but no sympathy was forthcoming. He sat at my desk, his arms crossed over his chest, watching me.

I got up. "Let her in while I put away her letters, will you?"

Hal glanced at the letters, then looked back at me with something akin to admiration.

"No speak English? Hal, do you mind?"

He laughed softly, looking suddenly cheerful. "My pleasure, Mowgli." He rose and crossed into the hallway. I heard him open the front door while I slid Kirsten's letters into my desk drawer.

A moment later, Hal ushered her into the living room.

Kirsten Strindberg looked around the room, then looked at me. Her face was pale, with every indication of recent tears. She clutched a handkerchief in her fist, and used it to push damp bangs off her face.

I love you dearly—please don't do this to me. I could feel my stomach knot; I hated her.

"Gary told me you'd rented this house," she complained, looking around. "I was going to wait till morning, but I saw your lights on." She hesitated. "What did

Gary say to you out there? I saw him open his eyes and say something to you."

My cousin stood in the doorway behind Kirsten. His expression said, *So that's it!*

"I really didn't hear. One of the firemen thought he said something about having fun at my office party."

"Why did you want to talk to Gary tonight?"

So she'd been wondering about that, had she? Enough to bring her over at two in the morning. "Lennart," I replied.

Kirsten's stubborn little mouth puckered, and she swayed on her feet. I felt no sympathy for her.

Apparently, Hal did. He said sharply, "Offer your guest a drink."

Grudgingly, I obeyed.

Kirsten blinked back tears. "Gary's all bruised up and he cracked two ribs."

Hal stepped up behind her and steered her to the couch. "That's painful, but it's not serious," he consoled her. "I've cracked ribs before."

I muttered, "Your own, I hope."

His glance left me unwithered. "Get her a drink."

"I don't want one," Kirsten said. She looked tired, but her posture remained perfect. "What are you doing back here, Laura?"

"I grew up here, remember?"

"But you always said—"

The buzzer sounded again. Hal bowed. "Shall I get it?"

I nodded, leaning against the wall. Champagne all afternoon, vodka all night. My brain felt numb, so did my lips and fingers.

I heard Hal telling someone he'd better wait outside, and I thought, *Yes, wait outside, preferably until Monday.*

When my cousin stepped back into the room, he looked unusually grave, even for him. He caught my eye and conveyed some emotion I was too drunk to read. Apology, possibly, or warning. "Some friends you've got, Mowgli," he said quietly.

"Who is it?"

"It's a fucking revolver, about two feet long."

"What?"

He nodded. "Stuck into my back, right now."

"I must be drunker than I thought."

Kirsten sputtered, "Is this a joke?"

Hal stumbled forward, and for the first time I saw a man standing behind him in the dark hallway. Apparently he'd given my cousin a little push with the barrel of the revolver.

I shook my head. "It can't be."

The newcomer grinned at me. He was a short man, stuffed into tight jeans, his shirt straining at the belly. He had round cheeks that dropped into a double chin, an acned forehead, fleshy lips, and sad brown eyes. His black hair was shoulder-length and thin, showing some scalp on top.

With Kirsten barking my name, and Hal staring grimly at the gun, I finally sobered up.

I crossed the room and snatched the revolver out of the man's hand. "You should know better than to carry around a weapon!"

The man's grin turned sheepish, and I heard Hal, behind me, expel his breath.

I pulled the man into the living room. "Get in here. Jesus! Did anyone see you with that thing?"

The man shook his head. "A guy down at the pier said to keep it for him for a while."

"Great. Why don't you just break into jail, and save the cops some trouble?"

Hal interjected, "Who is this guy?"

Kirsten began to hiccough.

"Don't you read the papers, Hal?"

"No. Who the hell—"

I turned to my cousin. "Henry Di Palma, Jr., meet Wallace Bean."

Hal's jaw dropped. Behind me, I heard Bean snicker.

I was about to add that Wally was not dangerous, when I remembered that he'd murdered two senators.

"Here, put this somewhere for me, would you?" I handed Hal the gun, and turned back to my client. "And Wally, don't you say another goddamned word to me about the gun, how you got it, or what you wanted it for, understand? Not while these people are here."

I glanced back to see what Hal had done with the gun, and found him still staring at me, his mouth twisted into a strange half smile. "You waiting for an invitation, Hal? Will you *please* get that thing out of plain view?"

For once, Hal's smile reached his eyes. He opened my desk drawer and dropped the gun in on top of Kirsten's letters.

That made four crimes I'd committed within six hours: breaking and entering, theft, tampering with possible evidence of a hit-and-run, and now, concealing what was very likely an unregistered firearm.

It was hard to believe I'd spent the afternoon charming judges.

I turned back to my unwelcome guest. "What are you doing here?"

"I heard that you came back to your hometown."

"So?"

"So I wanted to ask you something." Bean blushed. Even his ears turned scarlet.

"What?"

"It's private."

"No, it isn't," Hal said firmly.

Bean's expression clouded as he looked at Hal. "Who's he?"

"My cousin. Look, Wally, what do you want? It's late.

And I'm too drunk to be your lawyer tonight. Can't you come to my office in the—''

He shook his head, his eyes narrowing to woeful slits. ''It's personal.''

''Personal? Wally, I'm your *lawyer*. Our relationship is not 'personal.' ''

Bean's voice dropped to a husky pout. ''*Just* my lawyer?''

I looked at him and suddenly understood. That was all I needed—the puppy love of a psychopath. Hal stepped up beside me and put his arm around my shoulder.

''Where are you staying, Wally?'' I asked curtly.

''No place. I'm broke. I thought maybe I could—'' He looked meaningfully at my couch.

''No. You can't. But I'll lend you enough money to get you . . . wherever.'' It was a hell of a time to notice, but beneath my cousin's protective arm, I felt the contours of an exemplary body.

Bean's expression was transformed into that of a frustrated ten-year-old boy. He looked equally capable of violence or tears. Hal's arm tightened around me.

I vaguely noticed Kirsten standing up and moving across the room, but my attention was focused on Bean.

He was red as a tomato, his hands were shaking.

Then Kirsten Strindberg said, ''Get out of here.'' Her voice was tinged with hysteria.

Hal murmured, ''Careful, Laura, it's cocked,'' and I followed his gaze.

Kirsten stood directly behind my desk. Bean's revolver was in her hand.

''Put it down,'' I pleaded. ''What are you doing? Somebody's going to get hurt!''

I shook off Hal's arm, and started across the room to take the gun away from her. I was halfway there when Kirsten, inadvertently I think, pointed the gun at me.

I stopped in my tracks, heard Hal say, "Easy. There's no safety on a revolver!"

Kirsten and I made eye contact. She looked very pale. She also looked like she hated my guts.

In my most authoritative tone, I said, "Bean! Get the hell out of here right now!" Whatever Kirsten meant to do, she was not going to involve my client.

I heard a scramble of footsteps. Kirsten transferred her startled gaze to the hallway. I glanced behind me and found that Bean had taken my advice. I also found Hal staring at Kirsten, his expression intrigued. I turned to find that she'd put the gun down.

Right into my drawerful of letters.

She stared at them, open-mouthed.

When she looked up at me she looked absolutely demonic, she was so angry. "Where the hell did you—When did you—You could be disbarred for this!" she shrieked. "These are *my letters*!"

"In that case, you're welcome to them."

Behind me, Hal coughed back a chuckle.

"How did you get them?"

I was silent. That's rule number one of criminal defense: admit nothing.

"You *stole* them!" she accused, her cheeks flushing in patches. "I'll tell the police. I'll tell them—"

"That Lennart Strindberg didn't know how to drive a stick shift?"

That took the wind out of her sails. She gaped at me, her chin quivering, her brows puckered.

"Even if Lennart had known how to run a hose from the exhaust pipe to the interior of the car—"

"What are you doing?" Kirsten whispered.

"—he'd never have been able to get the Volkswagen all the way out to the jetty."

Kirsten's blue eyes filled with tears. She groped in the drawer, collecting her letters.

When she walked past me, I could smell her fragrance. It was light and pretty. Gary's favorite. I'd worn it for him all through high school.

A few seconds later, I heard the front door slam. Hal said, "Damn! You *are* something, Mowgli!"

"Yeah, sure. Thanks."

He twitched back a grin. "I didn't say *what*."

9

I WOKE UP up on the couch with no memory of having gone to sleep there. Hal was gone.

I phoned my papa.

"I came to visit you last night, but your lights were out, so I didn't knock."

"Everything all right?" He sounded worried.

"Yes. But listen, when I was leaving, pulling out of my parking space, I hit your car."

Silence.

I continued. "I don't think I did very much damage, just a few scratches, probably. I don't know. It was so dark out."

Papa's breathing had grown audible.

I waited—hoped—for an explosion of temper. None came. I added, "My insurance will cover it."

"Oh, well, if your insurance will cover it."

This was not the response I'd wanted. My stomach be-

gan to cramp in retaliation for the evening's excess of
vodka.

My papa said, "Your car? Is it all right?"

"Yes. Were you out in the Lincoln at around seven? I
thought I saw you."

"Seven? Earlier, I think. Henry took it to the supervisors' meeting last night. Laura . . ."

"Yes?"

"Nothing."

I hung up. My papa had seen me approach Gary Gleason at the office-warming, and he'd been standing close
enough to eavesdrop, if he'd cared to.

If so, he'd learned that Gary was coming to my house
at seven o'clock. He could have parked his Lincoln down
the street, and waited. He could have plowed Gary down
and made our rendezvous impossible.

But of course, he wouldn't have.

I phoned the hospital, and they put me through to Gary.

"Gleason," he responded groggily.

His voice sent a jolt of furious humiliation through me,
like an old song rekindling old feelings. "It's Laura. How
do you feel?"

"Drugged."

"You used to go to a lot of trouble to feel that way."

"Yeah."

I tried to think of something else to say, something appropriately conversational. I couldn't. "What did you say
to me last night?"

His tone was cautious. "You don't remember?"

"No."

There was a protracted silence, and I knew Gary was
weighing his options. He would tell me what he felt it
would be in his best interests for me to hear. That's how
he'd dealt with me as a husband; he'd be no more forthcoming as an adversary. But it would be useful, knowing
what Gary wanted me to believe.

He finally replied, "I don't remember, either."

"You don't know who hit you?"

"No."

"But you were hit from the front, weren't you?"

"The car came from behind me. I spun around when I heard it, but I was down and it was gone before I even realized what had happened."

My papa had been good to Gary when we were married. He'd gone out of his way to get to know him, despite Gary's long hair and radical views. And he'd decided Gary was an intelligent boy, a nascent professional, a good investment. He'd helped us with the rent, paid our junior college expenses, and bought us the secondhand Volkswagen.

If Gary had told me the truth the night before, then he was repaying my papa now with his silence.

I managed a few polite questions about his ailments, and wondered all the while if he meant to blackmail me.

It would be too bloody irritating if my plan were derailed at the last minute because Gary Gleason suddenly "remembered" who'd run him down.

And if he really hadn't seen the culprit—if he'd been nimble enough to say the one thing he knew he could use later to control me—I didn't see how the hell I could find out.

I felt myself grow hot with frustration. I'd only been back "home" a few days, and already things were going wrong.

I had to think of a way to neutralize Gary's advantage over me.

I glanced at my desk and remembered Kirsten standing there, the revolver in her hand.

I interrupted Gary's sleepy, "Thanks for calling," to say, "Your mistress pointed a gun at me last night." It wasn't much, but it was all I had.

"You mean Kirsten? What are you talking about?"

"I'm sure she'll tell you all about it." I hung up.

I crossed to the desk, wishing I'd remembered the revolver sooner. The damned thing was probably loaded;
not something I wanted sitting around my living room.

I opened the desk drawer.

It was empty.

10

I WAS FRANTIC. The revolver had Bean's fingerprints on
it, and there wasn't a cop, a journalist, or an average citizen (especially among Republicans) who didn't want to
see Bean in prison for *something* if not the senators' murder.

I was sure Hal had the gun. Kirsten and Bean were the
only other people who knew about it, and I couldn't imagine either of them sneaking into my house in the middle
of the night to get it. I grabbed my jacket, intending to
find my cousin and sock him in the jaw for worrying me
half to death.

I didn't get the chance. I heard someone pounding on
my door, and when I opened it two police detectives were
standing there, flashing their picture IDs at me.

I was politely told (not asked) to accompany them to
police headquarters.

The detectives drove me downtown to the courthouse,
where the police station and jail claimed the top two floors.

I sat by myself in a sparsely furnished cubicle that stank of disinfectant. My stomach reacted to the smell, and I shaded my eyes against the winking fluorescent light. I'd never mix champagne and vodka again.

For ten minutes I waited, afraid that I'd pushed Gary Gleason too far. I visualized my papa under arrest, his Lincoln under police impound.

The door finally opened and the pair of detectives ushered in a trim man with wavy silver hair, bright blue eyes, and a deeply cleft chin. His blue and white pin-striped shirt (no suit jacket) looked freshly starched. He introduced himself as Captain Loftus.

The name rang a bell.

I stood up, letting the captain pump my hand.

"We've all read about you, of course." He left it at that. Cops were not big fans of the TV-syndrome defense.

"Why am I here, Captain?"

But Loftus seemed determined to do a little socializing before getting down to business.

"My son went to school with you, Miss Di Palma. My son John."

John Loftus. Of course. He'd been a football star at my high school. He'd also been a reactionary airhead. John's idea of a good time had been shooting BBs through the Peace Center window. Gary had forgotten his pacifism long enough to come to blows with John because of it.

"I remember John. Is he still at the Volkswagen place?" After high school, John had become a mechanic. He'd repaired my old bug a few times; not often—animosity had inspired Gary to take up the wrench himself, whenever possible.

The captain looked away. "Killed in Vietnam." He pronounced it *Veet*-nam.

I sighed. It was too early in the morning to commiserate with strangers in a police station. "I'm sorry."

"Well, no need to be." There was a faint twang in his

voice. Oklahoma, probably; thousands of Okies had traded the dust bowl for the mud bowl. "It was a worthy cause, our country's honor. Me and his mother, may she rest in peace, we were proud of John."

"I'm sure," I murmured.

The skin around his eyes crinkled when he smiled. "Got to keep your perspective. My only boy, but . . ." He shrugged. "Veetnam was a lot better off under us than they are now with the Communists. That's a proven fact."

The police detectives exchanged glances; apparently they'd heard the captain ride this hobbyhorse before.

"Why am I here?" I repeated.

"Get Miss Di Palma a cup of coffee, will you, fellas?" He waited for the detectives to leave. "Sit down, sit down." He offered me a polished oak chair. San Francisco Police Department chairs tend to be scarred and sticky; I felt nostalgic for them.

I sat, and the captain did too.

"Miss Di Palma, we'd like to know when you last saw Wallace Bean."

Bean—I should have known. I wondered what the hell kind of trouble he'd gotten into this time.

"You brought me here to ask me about Wallace Bean? Is he in custody? Is he asking for me?" If so, the cops were violating Bean's right to counsel by questioning me about him; it might be enough to get the charges dismissed.

The captain hesitated, running a hand over the back of his head. "No. Not in custody exactly. But tell me, have you seen him recently? In this area?"

If he was just fishing for information about Bean, then he was exceeding the scope of his authority. My tone was sharp. "Why are you asking me about Bean?"

The captain leaned closer, searching my face with concerned eyes. "Well, I think we've got his corpse downstairs, Miss Di Palma."

I shook my head. Heard myself murmur, "What happened to him?"

He patted my hand. "Pretty darn ugly, I'm afraid. Twenty-two caliber bullet"—he turned his head and pointed to a spot at the base of his skull bone—"right about here. Come out just under the nose. Doesn't look like it coulda been self-inflicted."

"Someone shot him." The news magazines had all but predicted it. They'd labeled Bean the most unpopular man since Sirhan Sirhan. "Poor son of a bitch."

The captain slid his chair farther from mine. He appeared startled; possibly by my unladylike language, probably by my sympathy for Wally. He glanced at the door. "Where in the heck did Bill and Marty go? You look like you could use that coffee right about now."

"Have you arrested anyone?"

"No, 'fraid not. No weapon, no witnesses, no suspect, no nothing." He exhaled deeply.

"Where did you find Wally? Who called you?"

"You know the Lucky Logger?"

I nodded. A seedy bar in an unrenovated enclave behind the fish canneries.

"Owner found him in the alley when he put out the trash. I could run you over there right now. But maybe you're too upset—"

I stood up. "Let's go."

11

I IMAGINED WALLACE Bean on his knees in the dirty alley, being executed like some prisoner of war.

"It's the angle of the bullet tells us he was on his knees," Captain Loftus explained quietly. He extended his arm at a forty-five-degree angle, two fingers out like a gun barrel. "Somebody over him like this. You can see the way he fell." There was a foreshortened chalk outline between two dumpsters. "Fell forward, then sideways."

I looked away. A heavy layer of drizzle had collected on straggles of nasturtiums and geraniums growing among the broken beer bottles and sodden piles of litter. The back doors of bars, thrift stores, and bait shops were criss-crossed with yellow POLICE LINE streamers. Squad cars blocked either end of the crooked alley. Officers were turning away curious cannery workers in checked flannel and rubber boots.

"Mighty damp out here," the captain observed, wiping cold mist from his cheeks. "We can talk in the Logger, if that's all right with you." He motioned for a pair of policemen to resume whatever it was they'd been doing inside the dumpsters, and we went into the dark bar.

I slumped in a back booth, trying to ignore the faint but unmistakable stench of upchucked beer. The table top was heavily polyurethaned, smudged, and strewn with pretzel salt. The wall behind the captain was plastered with risqué bumper stickers.

Captain Loftus emptied a packet of imitation cream into his coffee. "You say Bean came to your house?"

My cup was chipped, stained black at the lip. I pushed it away. I'd have been happier with hair of the dog.

"It must have been close to two in the morning. Wally said he was broke. He wanted to sleep on my couch."

The captain frowned disapprovingly. A sticker above his head announced that *A Hard Man Is Good To Find*.

"I didn't let him. I offered to lend him some money, but . . ." I shrugged. "I try to keep a professional distance from my clients."

"You got to, your line of work. Did Bean take the money?"

"No." I hesitated. I hadn't mentioned my other guests, yet. I was reluctant to explain that Bean had fled because Kirsten had pulled a gun—Bean's gun—on him. I was even more reluctant to admit that the gun—entrusted to my care—had subsequently vanished. "Wally took offense. He walked out. He was in and out in less than ten minutes."

I hadn't lied; I'd just omitted certain details. Nor *could* I lie to the captain; the state bar would have my license if I did. I waited for Loftus to walk me through Bean's visit, utterance by utterance, occurrence by occurrence. I waited for him to force me to admit others had been present at the time; to ask me point-blank whether Bean had been armed.

Instead, he drank his coffee in thoughtful silence. I tried to conceal my surprise at his incompetence.

A few minutes later, one of the detectives I'd met that morning dashed into the bar. Even in the windowless gloom, the man's dishevelment and excitement were apparent. The captain joined him near the front door for a hasty conference that involved much gesticulating on the detective's part. The captain's back was to me, but I could see his gun hand shake as it patted his holstered hip.

When Loftus returned to the table, it was to excuse himself and offer me a police chauffeur.

"Did you find out something else about Wally?"

He shook his head gravely. "Too early to say. But we'll be in touch—you can count on it, Miss Di Palma."

12

IT SEEMED PROBABLE that Bean had crept back into my house while I slept, that he'd retrieved his gun, ultimately getting himself shot with it.

That meant big trouble for me. When a client leaves a deadly weapon with his lawyer for safekeeping, the lawyer's supposed to lock the damn thing away somewhere—not toss it into a drawer and forget about it. The state bar ethics committee, comprised of conservative old turds who'd publicly deplored the TV-syndrome defense, would be selling popcorn at my disciplinary proceeding.

There was always a chance, of course, that Bean had been killed with a different gun, and that my *cousin* had taken away Bean's gun.

If Hal had the gun, I'd strangle him for putting me in the untenable position of withholding information from the police. But at least I'd be able to get the thing back, wrap it in a handkerchief, take it to Captain Loftus, and grovel before him, apologizing for having "forgotten" to mention disarming Bean the night before.

I practically broke the sound barrier, speeding to my cousin's hovel.

And, in his usual unaccommodating manner, Hal was nowhere to be found.

His front door was unlocked, so I walked in. It was dark inside, with thin ribbons of daylight filtering through gaps in the boarded-up windows. I left the door open, to let in the pale light of an overcast morning.

The place looked like it had been recently swept, and the few tattered furnishings were spread with clean-looking blankets. But these efforts only accented the gloomy impersonality of the room, its absence of memorabilia. Even transients in flophouses tack up pictures, set out treasured objects, scavenge a few favorite magazines; Hal had done none of these things.

I wandered through Hal's house looking for some trace of him, but I found only the essentials of survival: in the kitchen, jars of food, bottled water, cheap wine; in the bedroom, a cot with no mattress or pillow, two thin blankets, a few piles of clothing; in the living room, a transistor radio, chairs, a few crate tables. There were kerosene lanterns here and there, but I had no reason to light them; there was nothing to see, nothing to do, in Hal's house.

It took less than five minutes to search for the gun. I got a flashlight out of my car and looked under the cot, in all the cupboards, in all the closets (now repositories for mouse droppings).

I was leaving when I thought of one last place to look. Since Hal had no key, he was forced to leave the front door unlocked. If he had any valuables, they'd certainly be hidden away.

I walked back through the house, shining my flashlight up at the ceiling. In the hallway, I found what I was looking for. Like most modern houses, this one had a ceiling panel that could be pushed aside for access to the rafters. I pulled a chair into the hall, tested it to see if it would bear my weight, and stood on it. I shifted the panel and shone the light up into the hole. On one side, I saw what looked like a sack. I tugged on it, and it fell down, nearly knocking me off my chair.

It was an army duffel bag, stenciled with Hal's last name. I carried it into the living room, and in the light of the open door, began looking through it.

Hal's army clothes were in there—a hat, a uniform, fatigues. It was in the uniform jacket that I found the Purple Heart. I pulled it out and held it up to the light; a heart-shaped medal with George Washington's profile on purple plastic. We'd never been notified, any of the family, that Hal had been wounded in the war. I wondered where, and how badly.

There were some papers under the uniform. I flipped through them. Topmost were two handwritten addresses: a veteran's hospital in Boston and the disability claims department of the Social Security Administration. The handwriting was loopy and feminine; definitely not Hal's.

The rest of the papers appeared to be photocopies of income tax returns, with W-2 forms attached. Over the years my cousin had been a bean picker, a janitor, a stable boy, a gardener, a quarryman, and just about every other sort of laborer, it seemed. Whatever his wartime injury, it obviously hadn't left him physically disabled.

I also learned that his yearly income had averaged four thousand dollars, that he'd never stayed long at one job, and that he'd traveled around the country a good deal. For some reason, laziness presumably, Hal had not filled out his own tax returns. Each was signed at the bottom by a different accountant in a different town.

Also in the duffel bag was an expired driver's license, showing Hal as he'd once been—plumper, with dimpled, uncreased cheeks and glossy black, well-cut hair. The license had expired in 1978, but a four-year extension, the kind they send you automatically if you don't get any tickets, was taped to the back. Apparently he hadn't gotten a second extension.

I groped around the emptied bag, and found one last object.

It was a small container, the kind used for prescription drugs. It was full of round, yellow pills. I had just enough time to read Hal's name on the label, to read the words *Thorazine, 500 mg: three times daily* before the container was snatched out of my hand.

I looked up to see Hal glowering at me, gripping the pills in a chafed, white-knuckled hand.

I stared up at him, too shocked to speak. Thorazine. They'd given Wallace Bean Thorazine at the state hospital. I'd asked the doctors about it and they'd explained that it was a powerful antipsychotic drug, used to sedate violent or uncontrolled patients. Bean's dosage had been 300 milligrams.

Hal's nostrils flared. His face, flushed from the cold morning, went slowly white.

For the first time in my life, I was afraid of my cousin. I stood hastily and backed away from him.

"Damn you," he whispered. He threw the pills against the wall so hard that the container shattered. "What the hell are you doing, snooping through my things?"

"I was looking for the gun, Hal. That's all." My God, what had happened to the good-looking, ordinary boy whose face had smiled at me from the old driver's license?

Hal frowned at the pills as they rolled and bounced across the floor, then he looked at the army uniform and the stack of papers beside the duffel bag. There was something about his face, something tired and wounded and plaintive, that undercut his anger.

"Hal?" I took a step toward him, extending my arm.

My cousin backed off. "What gun? You said you were looking for a gun."

"Wallace Bean's gun. Hal, did you take it?" I willed him to say yes.

Instead he said, "No. Why would I?"

"Keep it safe? Protect me?"

His smile was malevolent. "You don't need protecting, Laura; you need a good thrashing."

I sank into the nearest chair. "Well, if you're in the mood to see my life fall apart, you're certainly in luck."

Judging by the look on his face, he was indeed in the mood.

13

HAL DIDN'T KICK me out, and I made no move to leave. There were probably reporters on my doorstep by now. And if I went to my papa's house, I'd resume worrying that he'd tried to run over Gary Gleason.

I sat in Hal's armchair, brooding and shifting my weight to avoid broken springs.

Hal perched on a nearby crate, watching me, and doing some world-class brooding of his own. He waited a good, long time before breaking the silence. "So the gun's gone, is it?"

"Yes, the gun's gone is it." White, Sayres & Speck was fussy about their attorneys staying out of trouble; they might not want me back if the state bar initiated a disciplinary proceeding. And if my license was suspended, even for a short time, I was out of work for sure.

"So maybe Bean came back for it. Why don't you go ask him?"

"Meaning, why don't I get lost and leave you alone?"

The corner of Hal's mouth twitched, and he pressed his fingers to it. "Did I say that, Mowgli?"

"Stop this Mowgli crap, will you?"

I wondered if Hal might be lying about the gun. Maybe he'd taken it and gone after Wallace Bean. Maybe Hal hadn't liked having a gun pressed to his spine; maybe the war had made him a vengeful sort of person.

"What did you do last night after I passed out?"

Hal looked amused. "Nothing untoward, my dear. Did you think I'd been peeking under your sweater?"

"You didn't go out anywhere, did you?"

"I slept on your bed, if you must know. It seemed easier than carrying you upstairs so I could sleep on your couch."

"So you were upstairs. You weren't in the living room." I stood up and began pacing. "Someone, probably Bean, walked right into my goddamned house and took that gun."

"Too bad. It's a collector's item. You could have sold it and got a few precious bucks for—"

I whirled to face him. "A collector's item? You know what kind of gun it was?"

Hal nodded, looking mildly surprised by my reaction. "A real cowboy special. A Buntline Scout."

"What caliber?"

"Twenty-two. Why the interest in—"

"A twenty-two! I knew it, I just knew it." I could hear the tears in my voice. "They might as well rip up my law degree right now." I regarded Hal suspiciously. "How come you know so much about guns?"

"Spent a lot of time in the Southwest. Around a class of people you don't mix with."

"Bean pickers and janitors?"

Hal bristled. "I've had worse jobs than that, Laura."

"And I've defended poorer folks than you, Hal."

He cocked his head to one side. "I thought it took big money to pay your fees."

"Big money or no money. I do a lot of *pro bono* work."

Hal did not look convinced. "A girl who likes money as much as you do?"

"I'm a workaholic, cousin. I like to keep busy. Did Bean look affluent to you?"

Hal smiled. "Well. Surprise, surprise."

"Come on! Get up! We might as well go bite the bullet."

Hal stood up. "By all means. But what bullet are we—"

"We're going to the police."

Hal sat back down. "I thought lawyers weren't supposed to rat on their clients!"

"Rat on—Oh, I see. Didn't I tell you that Bean is dead?" I was relieved to see stark shock on Hal's face. "Probably murdered with a gun that was stolen out of my house while I was five feet away emitting vodka fumes. Now, come on, Hal, because I didn't mention the gun to the cops this morning, and the longer I wait, the worse it's going to look to the state bar."

Hal shook his head. "You're losing me. The state bar?"

"Is going to discipline me for failing to keep the weapon in a safe place. For letting a maniac waltz in and take a loaded gun out of my desk drawer."

"When you say discipline—"

"I mean draw and quarter, mop up the floor with, get revenge upon."

"Why revenge? I thought you were a big, important lawyer."

My patience was wearing thin. "Where have you been the last year, Hal? Sure, people admire my skill in getting Bean off scot-free; but they also hate me because they think I subverted the system. Christ, after the trial, the state legislature passed a law expressly prohibiting lawyers from asserting the TV-syndrome defense. You should read the legislative history, the floor debates. They make me sound like—" I cast about for an apt analogy, "Richard M. Nixon, for God's sake!"

Hal smiled, the biggest smile I'd seen on his face in thirteen years, probably. "I'll be damned."

"Yeah, me too, Hal." I clutched his arm and tried to pull him off his crate. "Now, come on. I like being a lawyer, and the quicker I put on a hair shirt, the better my chances of remaining one. So let's get going."

Hal remained seated, still smiling up at me. Gripping his arm, I became aware of a prodigious bicep.

In seventeen years of family dinner parties, I couldn't remember ever having noticed Hal's physique—only his obnoxious disparagement of my interests (ranging over the years from paper dolls to peace marches).

I released his arm, turning away. It had been too long since I'd slept with a man. I wished Sandy—

"Sandy!" I shrieked, looking in vain for a clock on Hal's damp walls. "I forgot about Sandy!"

"Who's Sandy?"

"My detective. He's been at the airport since nine."

"Your what?"

"Detective. For my law firm. Come on, hurry. We'll go get Sandy, and then we'll go talk to John goddamn Loftus's father."

14

IT WASN'T MUCH of an airport, and that's being charitable. There was a flight in every morning from San Francisco, and one out every afternoon, to San Francisco. There was also a flight in every evening from San Jose, en route to Seattle. The airport was on the foggiest hill in the county, so that no plane ever left or came in on time (my Uncle Henry had lobbied for this location, making some of his land-speculator friends in the Elks Club very rich). The building itself looked like an extra-large campground bathroom—all cement, very dark. It contained a ticket counter, a car rental concession, and an alcove of vending machines.

When Hal and I got there at eleven-thirty, it also contained one bored detective named Sander Arkelett.

Sandy was gazing out a window at wisps of fog, yawning. He was a very tall man with bad posture, a long face, sleepy blue eyes, and sand-colored hair. He'd become extraordinarily thin and pale since he'd been knifed in the belly six months earlier. He'd been chasing a purse-snatcher, and the boy had turned on Sandy and carved up his stomach before getting away. That's why Sandy was here now. He was still employed by the detective agency that White, Sayres & Speck used; but the agency, on a doctor's recommendation, had confined Sandy to delving through dull corporate records, and Sandy had gotten restless. It hadn't been hard to talk him into taking a leave of absence so he could sit in my showcase of an office and make my ex-husband envious.

When he saw me and Hal approaching, he glanced at his watch and shook his head.

"I'm sorry, Sandy. You'll forgive me when you hear—"

"Sure I will," he agreed, his eyelids drooping and the corners of his mouth lifting. His expression clearly broadcast his affection for me.

It brought Hal up short. He stopped, looking disconcerted.

I slipped my arm around Sander's waist, and began propelling him toward the door, explaining that Bean had been shot, and that I'd spent the morning with the cops.

Sandy crooked his arm around my neck and pressed my face against his lean rib cage. "You don't mind if I bring my bag along, surely?"

"Oh. No." I waited for him to go back to where he'd been standing and retrieve his soft-sided leather case. As he walked toward me with it, I noticed the girl at the car rental booth flash him a big, warm smile. Sander wasn't handsome, but he had that effect on women.

Hal noticed the smile too, and looked at Sandy appraisingly.

Sandy's shirt was rumpled and his trousers were baggy. His belt was wound to the tightest notch, with the end dangling. Desert boots and a worn anorak reinforced his air of languid shabbiness. And in spite of it—maybe because of it—Sandy was sexy.

I was the one who'd initiated the sexual part of our relationship. Sander was the one who'd confused things by falling in love.

"Okay, Wallace Bean," Sandy prompted, falling back into step with me.

As we walked out to the car, I told him the story, dwelling unhappily on the missing gun. It didn't occur to me to introduce Hal until it came time for the three of us to pile into my two-seater.

The two men shook hands, looking at one another with some interest and much wariness. My mind took a snapshot of their linked hands. Sandy's was long and smooth and pale, with a bit of smudged ink near one knuckle. Hal's was wide and rough and red at the knuckle. It made me angry. Sander had been wounded too; he'd been quite ill while his stomach healed. But he hadn't grown morbid and unhinged. He hadn't given up using his brain; he hadn't limited himself to menial jobs.

I told Hal to drive.

I settled myself on Sandy's lap, and my cousin roared out of the parking lot, tires squealing.

"Where to?" he asked.

"We've got to go tell the police about the gun."

Sandy wrapped his arms around me and nuzzled my neck. "Oh, I wouldn't worry too much about the gun, Laura."

I hunched my shoulders, twisting around to face him. I was in no mood to be nuzzled. "I lost the damn thing, Sandy. It was in my house last night, and there's a good chance it ended up killing Bean. And who the hell knows where it is now?"

Sander smiled lazily. He looked sleepy, but then, he usually did. "Nothing you tell the cops is going to help them find that gun. Comes right down to it, you don't know when it left, who it left with, or where it went—much less if it's the same gun that killed Bean. And when the police do find it, how's it going to help anybody, knowing you had it in your—"

"It's got all our fingerprints on it, Sandy. We all handled it last night, me and Hal and Bean and my goddamned ex-husband's girlfriend. If they find it, and I haven't already—"

"If your fingerprints survived Bean—or whoever—taking that gun and carrying it around; and then survived someone else firing it—" Sandy stroked my hair with a gentle hand. "No, I say forget it. Save yourself the aggravation."

I settled back into his lap and watched the scenery fly by; extravagantly tangled hillside on one side, waist-high dune grass on the other. A fierce wind chased away the fog, flattening the grass and blowing sand onto the two-lane highway. Hillsdale's evening (and only) newspaper would call it "a beautiful spring day."

Maybe Sandy had a point. I didn't really know anything that could help the homicide investigation. And if I kept my mouth shut, I might avoid the wolves at the state bar.

I glanced at my cousin, and found him smiling with ironic amusement. "I wouldn't get too comfortable, my dear," he murmured. "I don't think Kirsten Strindberg would mind seeing you squirm a little, do you?"

I groaned. Kirsten. Of course she'd want to see me squirm. Of course she'd go to the cops like a good citizen and tell them about the little drama in my living room the night before.

"I could strangle that woman!" I hissed.

Sandy looked glum and disapproving. And my obnoxious cousin laughed.

15

AT ONE O'CLOCK, Sandy clicked on the car radio, fiddling with the dial until he found a local news broadcast.

The newscaster, his voice throbbing with excitement, announced: *"Wallace Bean, who shot and killed two United States senators less than two years ago, was found shot to death himself in the predawn hours this morning, in an alley behind the Lucky Logger tavern on Pier Street. Police have so far refused to disclose whether the murder weapon has been found, or whether they have any suspects in custody."*

I turned to look at Sandy. He was squinting at the radio, tense with concentration.

The newscaster continued. *"Bean was released from the state mental hospital at Talmadge exactly two weeks ago, when doctors there certified that he was* not *insane. Bean was involuntarily committed eleven months and three weeks ago, after a jury found him not guilty, by reason of insanity, of the tragic shooting deaths of Senators Harley Hansen and Garth Dzhura. In a landmark legal effort, Bean's lawyer, Laura Di Palma, a former Hillsdale resident, convinced the five-man, seven-woman jury that Bean was brainwashed by watching too much violence on television."*

Sandy forestalled my usual protest with a placating, "I know, I know."

"*. . . recently opened a law office downtown. Police sources say they do not know whether Bean followed Miss Di Palma here, or whether he contacted, or meant to contact, her when he arrived. The police say they have no leads yet as to who shot Bean, or why. There has been some speculation in recent months that Bean risked being murdered by vigilantes once he got out of the mental hospital. Hospital administrators say he received numerous death threats from citizens outraged at the leniency of his punishment, and—*"

" 'Numerous.' " I repeated the understatement dryly. Death threats to me had been merely "numerous"; Bean's had outnumbered mine by a factor of twenty.

Hal looked at me, and veered into the wrong lane.

Sandy turned the volume up.

"*. . . and tragedy also struck a well-respected local couple last night and this morning. Local public defender Gary Gleason was struck by a hit-and-run driver in front of his Clarke Street residence last night at approximately six-forty p.m. He suffered lacerations and cracked ribs, and is reported in good condition at County Hospital. The driver has not been identified. Gleason's wife of ten years, Kirsten Strindberg—*"

"Wife?" Why had Kirsten kept Lennart's surname? And why hadn't Sandy mentioned the marriage when he'd briefed me?

"*. . . was found shot to death in their house—*"

"What!"

"*. . . by friends this morning. Police believe she had been dead less than two hours. KXTV News has reported that a twenty-two-caliber revolver was taken into evidence at the crime scene—*"

"Think we just found your gun," Sandy observed grimly.

". . . decline to speculate whether this was the weapon used in the attack on Strindberg, or whether Strindberg's murder is linked to Wallace Bean's."

Hal pulled over.

"Police have not yet determined whether any valuables were taken from the Strindberg-Gleason home, but say they have not ruled out—"

"My fingerprints are all over her vanity!" I felt Sandy stiffen, no doubt shocked at my self-absorption.

". . . say they are also exploring the possibility that the same person who ran down Gleason also murdered Strindberg."

The newscaster segued to a female colleague, who rehashed the news stories, giving them a gossipy, tabloid slant. Hal switched off the radio.

We sat in silence for a while. Hal spoke first. "Do we go to the police or not?"

My head ached, and it had grown stuffy in the car. The windows were steaming over. "I don't know."

"Could we talk about it over lunch?" Sandy suggested.

"We'd better make it my place, then." Hal put the car in gear. "We won't have a minute's peace, out in public with the notorious Ms. Di Palma today."

I told him I was touched by his concern.

16

WE DIDN'T MAKE it to Hal's house. A police cruiser pulled us over as we sped out toward the jetty.

The officer peered into the car. "Laura Di Palma?"

I nodded. Sandy's arm tightened around my waist.

"My orders are to stop your car and ask you to come to headquarters, Miss Di Palma."

"Can we follow you?"

"No. My orders are to bring you in." He turned his attention to Hal. "Driver's license, please."

"It expired."

The policeman's face, square and jowly, got that universal cop expression, a pale ghost of Clint Eastwood's "Make my day" look. "Out of the car," he ordered, standing back.

Hal obeyed.

The officer frisked him, pushing him up against the Mercedes with unnecessary violence. He informed my cousin that he'd have to wait at headquarters while they checked him for outstanding warrants. "Might take a few hours," he drawled unpleasantly. "The computer's got a lot on its mind today."

Then the cop came around to the passenger side of the car and opened the door for me.

I slid off Sandy's lap, saying, "Get some lunch, Arkelett, then pick us up at the courthouse. You can't miss it; it's the tallest building in the county.'' Four stories. ''If something comes up, I'll meet you at Hal's.'' The cop waited with obvious impatience while I gave Sandy directions to my cousin's hovel.

When we got to the police station, two officers led Hal away.

Captain Loftus himself escorted me to a pleasant, plant-filled office with a view of the old Rialto Theater. I saw from the marquee that it had been chopped into a four-theater complex and renamed UA Cinemas. I was outraged. I'd seen my first movie there. *Snow White*. Hal had thrown popcorn off the balcony.

''Sorry we had to stop your car.'' The captain started to sink into the chair behind the desk, then stood back up and came around to hold out a chair for me. I noticed that his sideburns were unfashionably long, and his silver waves a trifle wet, the way ladies in country bars like them. He probably turned a lot of hair-sprayed heads there.

''I heard the news on my radio.''

The captain crossed to the window. For a few seconds, he looked up at the steel-gray sky. Then he squared his shoulders and turned back to me. ''Just a few little things we need to clear up.'' His voice was weary but authoritative. ''You said Wallace Bean came to your house last night, asked to sleep on your couch, got offended when you offered him money, and then went away.'' He went back behind the desk, flicking a bit of loam off a philodendron leaf. ''Is there anything you could add to that statement to help us?''

I knew the captain hadn't gone to the trouble of getting my license plate number and ordering my car stopped just to ask for additional details. His men had found my fingerprints in Kirsten and Gary's house, probably on the vanity—maybe on the twenty-two. Or Gary had passed along my statement that Kirsten had pointed a gun at me.

"When I talked to you this morning, I didn't know that Wallace Bean was dead. My responsibility to him as a client prevented me from mentioning at that time"— Christ, I sounded like an affidavit—"that Bean was carrying a revolver when he came to my house." I tried to loosen up for the first hurdle: "When you did finally tell me Bean was dead, I was so stunned I forgot about the gun."

Captain Loftus put both hands on his desk top. I noticed a ridge of callus along his right index finger and thumb; chopping wood, I guessed. "Sometimes the stress of being here with us makes people a little forgetful, Miss Di Palma. That's why I asked you back this afternoon. You've had some time to relax and think about things." He turned his palms upward. It was a gesture I frequently used in negotiations, to suggest that I posed no threat and had nothing to hide. I wondered if the captain, too, had studied body language. "Did you happen to notice the make of the gun?"

"Some kind of long-barreled revolver. That's all I'm sure of. The only gun I'm familiar with is a forty-five automatic. Because of the Bean trial." I thought I noticed a quick twitch of anger on his face. "It definitely wasn't a forty-five."

"Anybody else see the gun, by chance?" His tone remained friendly; maybe just polite with an Oklahoma accent.

I told him Hal and Kirsten had been with me. When I mentioned Kirsten's name, Loftus's face went studiously blank.

"Tell you what, Miss Di Palma, why don't you just take your time and tell me what all happened."

I wondered why he hadn't asked me to do that five hours earlier.

I told him Bean had come to the door and forced Hal to let him in; that I'd chided Bean and taken the revolver away; that Bean had become upset when I'd refused to let him sleep on my couch; that Kirsten had panicked and sent Bean away at gunpoint.

Then I came to the second hurdle. Whatever I said about the disappearance of the gun, Loftus might be asked to repeat at a state bar disciplinary proceeding. I didn't dare admit that I'd been drunk and careless. "The gun was in my desk drawer; that's where Kirsten put it after Bean left. The desk doesn't lock, but I don't have a safe, or anything that can be secured. So I left the gun where it was, and I stayed in the living room all night. I slept on the couch, which is roughly opposite the desk—you have to walk by it to get to the desk. But when I woke up . . ."

The captain's blue eyes regarded me with mingled curiosity and sympathy.

"The first thing I did was check the desk. The gun was gone."

Loftus frowned and pursed his lips. "Had you locked your front door, Miss Di Palma?"

Drunk people don't worry about their front doors. "I really don't recall." That was one I owed Richard Nixon.

"And Mr. Henry Di Palma, Junior, did he leave after Mrs. Strindberg?"

"No. Since I planned to sleep on the couch, my cousin went upstairs and used my bed. He left first thing this morning."

The captain raised his grizzled gray brows. Who could have taken the gun more easily than someone already in the house, someone able to keep vigil and notice when I fell asleep? And if Loftus thought Hal was a made-to-order suspect now, wait until he met him. Hal had the kind of face only Charles Manson would trust.

I must have looked distressed. The captain offered a quiet homily. "I didn't think Bean or Mrs. Strindberg suffered much, Miss Di Palma. It's small comfort, I guess, but sometimes it's small comfort or none at all."

"Can you give me any details, Captain? The news said you found a gun—"

"A Buntline Scout—a great big old-fashioned Colt twenty-two. Funny." He scratched a sideburn with his knuckle. "You don't see those old guns too much anymore. I'm a collector myself, but I haven't seen a Scout— They're nowhere near as accurate as a rifle. And awful cumbersome for a handgun."

A Buntline Scout. That's what Hal had called Bean's gun. The gun I'd lost. "Where did you find it?"

"Living room." He nodded dreamily. "Real nice house. But I suppose you've been inside?"

No use denying it; I had almost certainly left fingerprints there. "Yes."

"Oh? Mrs. Strindberg show you around?"

I'd have given anything to answer, "Yes, she did." Kirsten was in no position to deny it. But Gary would tell the captain I hadn't been inside his house before last night's hit-and-run. Paramedics and neighbors would tell him I'd pulled up in my car right after the accident. Nurses would tell him Kirsten had arrived at the hospital with Gary, and remained there until the wee hours—until she'd come to see me at my house, in fact. So if I told Captain Loftus I'd paid Kirsten a call, he would necessarily conclude I'd done so early this morning—when she was being murdered.

"No, she didn't," I admitted reluctantly. "When she went to the hospital with her husband, she left her front door open—not just unlocked, but ajar. I went over there to lock up for her." I met his eye. I'm good at looking people in the eye; it's a fine technique to use on mistrustful jurors. "You probably know that Gary and I were married once."

He nodded.

"Well, I was curious." I smiled apologetically. "I just

wanted to take a peek, you know? I did tell Kirsten about it later, when she came to my house."

"I see." His forehead crinkled sympathetically. "And Mr. Gleason's business office?"

"I've never been there."

"Mmm-hm. I understand there's a little matter of some papers?"

I was stunned. Who could have told the police about the letters? I couldn't imagine Kirsten rousing Gary in the middle of the night to complain that I'd stolen them. Besides, when I'd phoned Gary this morning, he'd seemed perplexed by my reference to a gun. If Kirsten *had* called him, she would surely have mentioned the encounter with Bean. If Gary didn't know about Bean, then he didn't know about the letters, either.

And if Gary hadn't told the police about the letters, no one had.

Which meant they'd played some part in Kirsten's murder. Perhaps she'd been rereading them when the killer interrupted her. The letters mentioned me, of course: Gary's referred to me guiltily; Lennart's regretted being troubled with my love.

But I didn't think the police knew the letters had ever been in my possession.

So I took a chance. It would have been too mortifying, admitting that I'd stolen my rival's love letters. I said, "No. I don't know what you mean. There might have been some papers on a desk or table when I walked through the house, but I was just getting an impression of my ex-husband's life, Captain. Just being curious. I invaded his privacy, I know—but not to the extent of going through his mail, or anything like that."

The captain nodded reassuringly. "Well, I suppose that's it for right now, then."

For a moment I just sat there, trying to hide my surprise. The casualness of his interrogation, his trust-me manner, his tardiness in asking me key questions: maybe he was just a nice, inefficient, small-town cop.

Or maybe he was too smart to use techniques a criminal lawyer would recognize.

17

I WAS MOBBED as soon as I stepped out into the afternoon wind. I'd hoped no one would notice me in my jeans and sweater; reporters were accustomed to seeing me in wool suits. But all it took was one excited, "There's Bean's lawyer!" and cameras began clicking and whirring.

The way I looked, I'd rather have faced a firing squad than a camera. At the best of times, TV makes me look ten pounds heavier, and makes me sound like Julia Child with a head cold.

I recognized a couple of news crews; they'd wasted no time racing up from San Francisco. I said hello to a handsome, well-dressed black reporter from KRON (gay, like every other handsome, well-dressed man in San Francisco); "How are you?" to a skinny *Chronicle* reporter who reeked of garlic, as usual; and "Still behind the camera?" to a high-heeled blonde on her way (she hoped) to becoming the KPIX weather girl. A pudgy woman in polyester thrust herself forward, gushing, "Laura, remember me? Judy Britt? From high school?" She giggled that she was with the *Hillsdale Union-Messenger* now, and I felt a wave of horrified pity for her.

The KRON reporter expertly elbowed her aside, saying, "Can we have a statement, Miss Di Palma?"

"Wallace Bean was prosecuted to the full extent of the law, and this sort of vigilante justice is an insult to the legitimate judicial process," I declared pompously. The statement lacked depth, but it would strike the right note on TV. I concluded with the mandatory, "I have no other comment, pending results of the police investigation."

Notwithstanding, I was barraged with questions: "Did Bean follow you here?" "Did he call you?" "Did you see him?" "Why did he come here?" "Did anyone come with him?" "Did you know Jeanne Dixon predicted the murder?" "What about this other murder?" "Wasn't Kirsten Strindberg married to your ex-husband?" "Are you a suspect, Ms. Di Palma?" One woman shouted, "Was Bean in love with you?" and someone shouted even louder, "Do you feel morally responsible for his death?"

I tried to break through the throng, but the reporters weren't budging. The garlic-eater from the *Chronicle* moaned, "Be a pal, Laura. What do you *really* think is going on here?"

I tried to push past him, but the aspiring weather girl was right there, shoving her camera in my face. Once again, and from every side, it was, *Did he call you? Did you see him? Did they show you his dead body? Do you regret getting him acquitted?*

My cousin Hal saved the day (my day, anyway) by pushing his way through to me. He put his arm around me and bulldozed me out of the crowd, showing little regard for expensive camera equipment. He shepherded me to a waiting taxi, and when I protested that we were supposed to meet Sandy, he shouted over the cacophony of questions, "Get out of here! I'll wait for him." He slammed the door

shut, glancing up at what was fast becoming a sky full of
nimbus clouds.

The cab driver squinted at me curiously. "Are you on
TV or something?"

"I'm Sophia Loren's daughter."

"Sure!" the driver exclaimed. "Hell, you look like her!
Like she did in the movie about the fountain!"

Just what I needed, a blind cab driver. "Take me to
County Hospital, would you?"

Getting in to see Gary was tricky. The nurse wanted the
okay of a doctor who had apparently vanished from the
face of the earth. I ended up handing her a slip of paper
with seven randomly selected digits on it. "The doctor's
at this number. He says I can go in."

"Well, he's the boss." She didn't even glance at the
paper. Instead she leaned across the file-strewn counter
and confided, "It's just a police thing, anyway. He could
have gone home this morning."

Behind her, another nurse stopped filing. "Janet! Didn't
you hear about his wife?"

I left them to their gossip, and went to find Gary's room.
I passed a door marked ADMINISTRATIVE NURSE, and recognized the name on the plate: someone I'd known in high
school, someone who'd dreamed of moving to Paris. I felt
a claustrophobic chill. I wanted to shout from the rooftops
that I wasn't really back to stay; that I wasn't like my
lumpen classmates; that I'd never be content to gather
small-town moss.

Gary's room heightened my desire to flee. The linoleum
was so old it was no longer capable of looking clean. The
walls were painted an age-darkened tan, and the windows
showed signs of crumbling at the sills.

Gary lay in bed looking utterly blank—a startling departure from his usual thoughtful frown and appraising
eyes.

He noticed me. His mouth twisted.

I said, "I heard about Kirsten."

"Why'd you come back?" His whisper was bitter.

I pulled a chair up to his bed. "A friend of mine is a private detective. He came up here on a case a couple of months ago, and I asked him to find out if Lennart still lived here." Actually, Sandy had volunteered to find out what had become of Lennart; I'd told him about the thwarted affair one night when he'd inquired why my marriage had broken up. "He came back and told me Lennart had—died. That he'd run a hose from the exhaust pipe—" I closed my eyes.

I opened them to find Gary watching me, his eyes bright and resentful.

I continued. "My friend brought me a photocopy of Lennart's obituary. That's how I found out he'd died in our—in the old VW. That he'd supposedly driven it out to the jetty and—" I looked at Gary's hand, where it rested on the hospital sheet. He wore a broad white-gold wedding band. The bastard. "You know damned well Lennart couldn't drive that car. You tried yourself to teach him to work the stick shift and clutch, and you—" I swallowed. "You came home laughing about what a klutz he was. You said he'd never learn."

"What do you want me to say? I was wrong. He learned. He made it out to the jetty."

"I was waiting for Lennart that night. I was at the Trade Winds Motel. We were going to go to San Francisco together. The obituary said Lennart had a suitcase with him."

Gary's scowl deepened. "Did you look for Lennart when he didn't show up? Try to find out why he didn't meet you?"

"No. Because Lennart phoned me at the motel."

Gary started to say something.

I cut him off. "At midnight."

"At midnight," he repeated. "The police said—"

"Right. I got a call from Lennart fifteen minutes after he died."

Lennart Strindberg had already been dead at 11:45, when a police cruiser noticed the Volkswagen sitting at the foot of the jetty with its lights out and its motor running. It was all in the police report.

"He told me that he and Kirsten were reconciling, and that he wouldn't be coming with me, after all."

"You didn't—The voice didn't sound odd?"

"I don't remember thinking so. But I was pretty emotional."

Gary closed his eyes. I became aware of a quiet tap-tap-tap on the window behind me. Rain.

"You knew Lennart's voice well enough to imitate it," I pointed out. It had been an unusual voice, not quite free of a German accent. "And you knew the situation. You knew what to say."

Gary's eyes opened. "What are you—?"

"When I found out how Lennart died, I knew he'd been murdered."

Gary's lips formed the word "no," but no sound came out.

"And I came here to do you—you and Kirsten—as much harm as I possibly could."

"You thought me and Kirsten—? Me and *Kirsten*?" Gary's face bore traces of the righteous, martyred outrage he'd worn to protest marches in the early days of our marriage. "She'd been with him two years. I considered him a good friend."

It was all I could do not to spit in his face, despite his present troubles. He'd slept with his "good friend's" wife for five months before Lennart and I found out about it.

"The money Kirsten inherited from Lennart put you through college and law school," I reminded him. Sandy had done some research. Lennart had been the eldest son of a deceased German industrialist. The industrialist had left a trust fund for Lennart's nine-year-old brother Dieter, and he'd left Lennart money and an office building in the heart of San Francisco's financial district. A few weeks before his supposed suicide by carbon monoxide inhalation, Lennart had willed everything to Kirsten.

Gary's eyes narrowed; his nostrils flared. But he couldn't deny that Lennart's death had been a financial blessing.

And up until that afternoon, when I'd learned Kirsten had been murdered, I'd have bet my soul that she and Gary had killed Lennart for his money.

Now, with Gary in the hospital and Kirsten dead, I wasn't so sure.

18

THE WIND WHIPPED freezing rain in several directions at once. An umbrella would have been no match for it; I'd already passed one tumbling down the street, inside out and broken like a giant wounded bat. A raincoat would have been better, but it wouldn't have kept me dry below the knee. I knew; I'd spent years of my life peeling wet tights off the clammy gooseflesh of my legs.

I walked past boxy Victorians with fat, solitary palms in front, past block-long stretches of sidewalk-ringed ravine, past ranch-style houses landscaped with skinny redwoods, past shabby bungalows with pickups in their muddy yards. My glove-leather flats were waterlogged; my pants drank in mud from hem to thigh; my sweater was sodden; my hair was beaten into limply corkscrewed cascades. All around me, snails slid like slow boats over the eddying rainwater.

The last time I'd walked the streets of my hometown, I'd been crying so hard the rain hadn't mattered.

That day, Gary had arranged an excursion to Fern Canyon: he and I, Lennart and Kirsten. At the last minute, he'd begged off to study for a junior college Bio 101 exam. When Kirsten begged off too, I was pleased. A day alone with Lennart. I sneaked glances at his sensitive profile every time I shifted the VW's gears.

But the car had broken down halfway to the canyon, beside a lagoon where elk liked to congregate. Lennart and I hiked to a phone and called for a tow truck. On a whim, I took his hand. He didn't pull it away, but he didn't squeeze back, either. We went back to wait with the elk. Their antlers spanned ten feet, but they were dumb, unaggressive animals. We fed them brambles.

It was raining by the time John Loftus pulled up in his tow truck. He dropped us off at my house, taking the VW on to the repair shop.

The apartment door was locked, for once. I let us in with my key. And we found them on the living-room floor, on the sheepskin rug my mother had bought me when I was a baby. The rug I'd always kept clean and brushed, draped over a chair.

Kirsten had been on top.

"Damn you!" I whispered to the rain, fourteen years too late. "Damn you!"

Then, I'd said nothing. I'd turned tail and run.

"I should have said something!" I should have forced her to leap off him and cover herself up. I should have made him cringe and grovel in apology. I should have made them cry.

Instead, I'd left them on my sheepskin (and in my memory) *in medias res.*

I'd stumbled outside, right behind Lennart. In time to witness his awkward, arm-flailing dash into the rain.

I pushed soaked hair out of my eyes. I had walked a long time that day with no awareness of the cold. Not so today.

I found a phone booth and shivered in it, dialing with numb fingers. I begged the taxi company to hurry.

The day of the sheepskin, I'd phoned Jay Bartoli for a ride. In my fury, I'd insisted he take me home and make love to me. Lying on my sheepskin in a fever of mortification, I learned the whole truth. "We all figured you knew. They've been hot and heavy five, six months already," Jay had announced casually. And I'd shrieked that I didn't care; that I was in love with someone else anyway.

That evening, I'd thrown Gary's clothes—and my mother's sheepskin—outside to molder in the freezing mud. No one showed up to stop me. A note on the kitchen table read: "I think it would be best if I split for a while."

In the wee hours of the morning, Lennart had come to see me. Lennart, with his necessary manners. He was too gallant—maybe too unhappy—to refuse my love.

Two days later, Gary had finally taken his sodden things out of the yard. I was standing behind a barely-parted curtain, paralyzed by my own venom. I watched him pile wet clothes into the newly overhauled VW that my papa had paid for, and that I never saw again.

A week later, Lennart Strindberg died in that car.

Fourteen years later, I found out he was dead.

I hadn't planned to accuse Gary and Kirsten of Lennart's murder, not publicly; the evidence was too cold, too flimsy. But I'd looked forward to *threatening* to do it, just as I'd looked forward to threatening to put Gary out of business. I didn't run from confrontation, not anymore.

Gary Gleason was smart enough to know that an accusation of murder, coming from me, would blossom into a media event. He wouldn't want to subject himself and Kirsten to the publicity—and risk—of an investigation.

So I'd been prepared to offer the bastard a choice: his reputation and his livelihood, or Kirsten. If he agreed to walk out on Kirsten without telling her why, I'd keep quiet about Lennart's inability to drive the Volkswagen. I'd also tear up the public defender contract, and move back to San Francisco.

And if he hesitated to leave his true love? I had one last threat—one I was prepared to carry out. I would track down Lennart's brother, Dieter, and offer him the gift of my legal services.

Dieter had been only a boy, living with his legal guardian in Germany, when Lennart died. Lennart's will, leaving everything to Kirsten, had cheated Dieter of his father's American holdings—including the fast-appreciating San Francisco building where White, Sayres & Speck had their offices.

By my calculation, Dieter had recently attained his majority. If I asserted that his guardian had been derelict in his fiduciary duty, Dieter could avoid the statute of limitations and challenge Lennart's will.

A murderess can't inherit from her victim; and in probate court, the standard for proving murder is not "beyond a reasonable doubt," as it is in criminal court. If six out of nine jurors believed Kirsten had "more likely than not" conspired to murder Lennart, then Lennart's property would revert to his brother Dieter under the laws of intestate succession.

Even if Gary did not mind risking his career and his reputation, I thought he would balk at putting Kirsten's fortune on the line.

Gary and Kirsten's forced separation was to have been my meager memorial to Lennart Strindberg.

But that end had been achieved by someone else—achieved in such a way that I could take no satisfaction in it. I was no longer certain my ex-husband deserved it; no longer certain Gary Gleason had killed Lennart Strindberg.

19

THE TAXI DROPPED me at Hal's house, where I expected to find him and Sandy.

I didn't notice until after the cab pulled away ("You *sure* this is the right place, lady?") that my Mercedes wasn't parked in the driveway.

I wandered through the leaky house, feeling marooned. It was a hell of a walk back to the nearest phone. I could hear waves smashing over the jetty, could feel the foundation shudder beneath the floorboards.

The house was as cold as a refrigerator, and much damper. I couldn't open the door for light because the wind and water whipped in. I searched the kitchen for matches to light the lanterns, but I didn't find any.

I groped my way back to Hal's bedroom, and shucked my icy sweater. I'd just put on one of Hal's fuzz-balled pullovers when I heard a scraping sound and felt a blast of cold air. The front door had opened. I was about to call out my cousin's name, when I saw a gleam of artificial light on the damp floor.

A flashlight. That morning I'd searched through Hal's possessions. A flashlight had not been among them.

Maybe it was the sound of the storm beating against the boarded-up window, maybe it was the darkness of the deteriorating house. Something frightened me into unwonted caution. I snatched up my wet sweater and hid behind the open door of Hal's room, shielded from view.

A moment later, light swept the room. It picked out Hal's cot, his piles of clothes, the cracks in the exterior walls, the spreading puddle beneath the window where the wet boards dripped.

It was a long moment before the flashlight turned away and the room was dark again. I peered through the crack between the open door and the door frame, and saw the light bob down the hallway, silhouetting a form in a big hooded jacket.

Then I heard footsteps at the other end of the house, in the living room. The flashlight swung around, blinding me for a moment. Then it was clicked off.

There was little natural light in the hallway, just a bit that filtered through the boarded-up windows in adjoining bedrooms. But as the footsteps grew louder, I could see the hooded figure shift the flashlight from his right hand to his left, slip his hand under his jacket, and pull out another flashlight-sized object.

I glanced toward the living room, and saw the outline of a tall man with wild hair—my cousin Hal. As I watched him approach the hallway, my brain made sense of what I'd just seen the man with the flashlight do.

"Hal!" I shouted. "He's got a gun!"

My cousin jarred to a stop, then lunged forward into the hall.

The shots sounded like cannon blasts. I watched Hal dive to the ground.

I rushed from my hiding place, throwing myself on top

of him. There was a sound like a donkey braying—me, screaming.

Hal tried to wriggle out from under me, cursing.

"Are you shot? Are you hurt?" I quavered.

Apparently he was not: he scrambled to his feet, knocking me over. Then he dashed toward the back of the house, toward the kitchen door.

I rose shakily and followed. I found Hall staring out at a wall of rain. He slammed the door, with a resounding, "Shit!"

He turned to me, glowering, strands of gray and black hair plastered to his forehead, his clothes dripping.

He grabbed a lantern from a hook near the door, catching me by the wrist and pulling me back down the hall. When we reached the bedroom, he dug some matches out of his pocket and lit the lantern. He held it up to the door.

"That's what I thought," he muttered.

I stood behind him, trembling with cold and shock, peering at the door from behind his back. "What is it?"

"Bullet holes, Mowgli." He turned to face me. "It was you—your voice—he shot at, not me."

20

HAL CHOPPED UP some driftwood and a three-legged chair, and built a fire. I huddled in front of it while he went to change into dry clothes.

I'd barely begun to get warm when I heard the spinning tires of a car in the rain. I stood up, staring at the front door. I almost swooned, I was so damned scared. Nobody had ever taken a shot at me before, and I didn't like it.

I ran to Hal's bedroom. If I was going to face the man in the hooded jacket again, I wanted Hal with me. I didn't think twice about flinging the door open.

Hal stood near his cot, toweling his hair dry, not a stitch of clothing on his body.

And what a body. Years of physical labor had made his chest, shoulders, and arms bulge with muscle. His belly was tight, his hips lean, his thighs tough. When I first opened the door he looked surprised. When I glanced back up at his face, he'd dropped the towel and was smiling at me.

I was embarrassed. "I heard a car."

He stepped closer, putting his hands on my waist. He smiled down at me. It was a beautiful smile, unclouded by animosity or cynicism, for once. I put my palms against his damp chest, feeling his muscles ripple as his arms circled me.

"Thanks for playing human shield," Hal murmured in my ear.

He kissed me in a very uncousinly way.

And I kissed him back, sliding my fingers through his hair.

It didn't register until later that my fingers encountered scar tissue on my cousin's scalp. Enough to make his hair stick out at odd angles no matter how well-cut it might be.

Hal said, "You're right about the car, Mowgli."

I blinked up at him. "The car?"

He nodded. "I heard a car door slam. You want to know who I think it is?" Someone began pounding on the front door. "I think it's probably Sandy."

My cousin slid his hand under my borrowed sweater.

We heard the front door open, and my cousin smiled down at me, mischievously.

I backed away, shaking from an excess of hormones. Then I turned and left the room, adjusting the sweater.

I almost collided with Sandy where the hallway met the living room. His slacks were dark with rain from the thigh down, and he carried a dripping anorak. He was wiping his cheeks with his sleeve when he saw me.

He was beginning to grin, when he glanced behind me and frowned. I looked over my shoulder and saw Hal's bedroom door close.

"Where have you been, Sandy?" I resolutely took his arm and led him to the living room. "I've got a lot to tell you."

I told him about the man who'd shot at me.

Sandy watched me solemnly, his damp, tousled hair gleaming with auburn highlights in the firelight.

Hal joined us, wearing frayed jeans and a tight turtle-neck. He glanced at me with the hint of a smile on his face.

I looked at Sandy. His eyes narrowed as he watched Hal; he'd noticed that smile too. His tone was less than friendly when he asked Hal, "Why didn't you go after the guy? He must have come in a car. If you'd gotten a look at it, we'd have something to go on."

My cousin regarded him coldly. "And leave Laura alone in the house? With no guarantee the guy wouldn't circle around front and come back inside?"

The two men exchanged frosty looks. Hal knelt to settle some sticks of driftwood onto the fire.

Sandy turned back to me, asking me to describe the figure again. While I talked, he frowned at my cousin's back.

"Not much to go on," he mused.

"No," I agreed. "Did you go to my house, Sandy?

Where were you? Did Hal explain why I left the court-house?''

"I waited for you a while," Hal muttered, turning to face Sandy. "When you didn't show, I walked home."

"Walked? All this way?"

"No driver's license, remember?"

"Why not?"

My cousin shrugged. "Didn't feel like taking the exam."

Determined to court every inconvenience, my cousin.

I asked again, "Where did you go, Sandy?"

"Well, as a matter of fact, I learned a little something that might interest you." Sandy slumped in his chair, crossing his legs at the ankles. "I bought a lady policeman some lunch. Told her some of my war stories from when I was on the force in L.A."

"You used to be a cop?" It was the first I'd heard of it.

His eyelids drooped. "A long time ago."

Hal was curt. "So what did you find out?"

Sandy sat up again, looking at him. "You might find this interesting, too. The gun they found at the Gleason house was a twenty-two, all right, but they're not positive it's the gun that killed Bean."

I was surprised. "I thought they had a lot of sophisti-cated tests—"

Sandy shook his head. "Basically, they just fire a bullet out of a gun and see if the little scratches on it match the scratches on the bullet that did the killing. But this piece is an oldie. It's jammed. They sent it down to the city, but the ballistics people there can't get it to fire, either. All they can say for sure is that it *was* fired, fairly recently. The bullet they pulled out of Bean had the right kind of markings—same spin. It definitely went through some kind of long-barreled twenty-two. And since they found one at Gleason's, they're guessing it's the murder weapon."

Hal asked, "Did it match the bullet they took out of—"

Sandy interrupted. "I was getting to that. They pulled a thirty-eight caliber out of Strindberg. We've either got two killers here, or one killer with two—"

Hal interjected, "A thirty-eight? I suppose you carry a Detective Special."

Sandy looked irritated. "*When* I carry a gun, which is almost never."

"A 'Detective Special'?" I was lost.

Sandy said, "It's a snub-nosed Colt that a lot of cops and private detectives use. Them and a hell of a lot of other people besides. It happens to be a very popular handgun."

"Where exactly did the cops find the twenty-two? Did your lunch date tell you?" There was a snide undercurrent in Hal's tone, but I didn't know what it meant.

"The twenty-two was in a drawer."

"With some letters?" I asked him.

Hal's face lit with interest. "Cops asking you about your letters, Mowgli?"

Sandy glanced from Hal to me. He looked piqued, like someone outside of an inside joke. "She didn't say anything about any letters."

It was just like my goddamned cousin to refer to them as "my" letters. "Letters to Kirsten from Gary and Lennart," I explained. "The police captain asked me about them this morning, and I wondered why."

Sandy continued to watch me, and I felt myself flush. As if to confirm Sandy's impression that I was being less than candid, Hal chuckled as he turned to grab a lantern.

Motioning for us to follow, he led the way into his room. He closed the door and held the lantern so we could see what the bullets had done to the cheap door. Pieces of veneer had splintered off, leaving ragged, squarish holes.

Then he held the lantern up to the wall behind the door,

where I'd been standing. A foot above the top of my head there were two small craters where the Sheetrock had collapsed.

"Not much of a marksman." Sandy pulled out his pocketknife. He dug a bullet out of the wall, where it had lodged in a stud. He held it in his palm, in the full light of the lantern.

"It's a thirty-eight all right," he confirmed.

21

IT WAS TWILIGHT by the time the three of us got to Clarke Street. The rain had stopped, leaving the air clear and icy. Torrents of water gushed along either side of the street, disappearing into cavernous, roaring pipes at the corners. Down the block from my house, an old man unclogged his rain gutter with a stick, while his wife held the ladder for him. Another neighbor pulled a plastic tent off her rain-beaten daffodils. A toddler sat on a wet porch, running his fingers over the slick wood, then licking them.

At my end of the block, all traces of normalcy vanished. Half a dozen reporters were encamped on my front steps, and at least as many lounged in logoed vans and station wagons. Wallace Bean had been in the news for over two years, omnipresent at times, invisible at others, like a national case of cold sores. Murdered—executed—he was once again the lead story, film at eleven. And I'd been his lawyer. He died in my hometown. The reporters wanted a statement.

I noticed the handsome KRON reporter interviewing someone—a neighbor, presumably—in front of Gary Gleason's house. A yellow plastic streamer kept them off the lawn, and a row of police cars kept gawkers from congregating in front. A second murder hours after Bean's, in the same small town. The press was bound to exploit every innuendo.

Judy Britt waved to me as I climbed out of the Mercedes, and suddenly the news vans began to empty. The reporters on my porch leapt to their feet; cameras were hoisted, lights were hastily clamped to tripods, microphones and tape recorders were adjusted. I pushed my way through to my front steps, saying, "No comment. No statement now."

That didn't stop the questions. "Did Bean contact you?" "What was Bean doing here?" "Do you think he was murdered by right-wing vigilantes?" And more personal questions: "Is it coincidence that you live across the street from Kirsten Strindberg?" "Do you know anything about her murder?" "Did she know Wallace Bean?" "Wasn't she married to your ex-husband?" "Did your ex-husband ask you to move here?" "Did he know Bean?" "Was he jealous of Bean?" "Was Strindberg jealous of you?" "Is your presence tied to her murder?" "Are you still in love with your ex-husband?"

"Hell no!" I blurted in response to the last. The reporters laughed, and I began elbowing through them, climbing the steps to my front door, Hal and Sandy right behind me.

Then Judy Britt tossed a morsel of information to the piranhas. "Gleason left you for Strindberg, didn't he?"

She stood between me and my front door, looking utterly dowdy in maroon polyester. Her hair was in a limp pageboy, her double chin met her collar. And I finally remembered her. "You petitioned the principal to keep antiwar protests off campus." A swell of reporters pushed me up against her. I smelled Chanel No. 5; cheap and passé—it figured.

I elbowed her to one side and unlocked my door. Talking to the press only invites garbled confusion; the Bean trial had taught me that. Britt would write what she wanted to write, and the others would misconstrue it as they chose to misconstrue it. Over the hubbub, the KRON reporter boomed, "Is it true? Did your husband leave you for Strindberg?"

I wheeled around, pushing my startled cousin aside. "No, he didn't!" I announced to the microphones and cameras. "I was in love with someone—"

Judy Britt smirked, and I felt myself teeter on the brink of indiscretion. Hal gave me a firm backward push, shielding me from view with his body. Before I could protest, he'd backed me into the house, and Sandy had closed the door behind us.

Neither man said anything. Hal stepped into the living room; I watched him pour vodka into last night's glass. Sandy pulled a telephone credit card out of his wallet, waving it at me inquiringly.

I pointed to the hallway phone, then fled upstairs.

A hot shower helped. So did dry clothes.

I was trying to coerce my hair into tidiness, when I heard a knock at the back door.

My bedroom window faced the overgrown plot of mud in back. I opened it and leaned out, wondering if some enterprising reporter had climbed my back fence.

I saw a man in a business suit, but it was too dark to see who it was until the back door opened, bathing him in light.

It was my Uncle Henry.

Hal stepped out onto the porch, closing the door behind

him. I heard a sound I never thought I'd hear: I heard my Uncle Henry cry.

Hal, a good eight inches taller than his short, stocky father, watched him. He kept his distance, saying nothing.

Slowly my Uncle Henry regained control of himself. He stood facing his son (facing me, too, had he looked up), mopping his eyes with a handkerchief. He swayed slightly; I wondered if he'd been drinking.

My uncle said, "You should have told me, too."

Hal's tone was dry. "*I* didn't tell anyone."

My uncle's voice became hushed, confiding. "I'd have looked after you, hired someone to help you with—"

"I didn't need help."

"Henry, please. I'm your father; let me help you now. It's no disgrace to be handicapped in this day and—"

"I'm *not* handicapped. If you want to see handicapped go to the goddamned vets' hospital sometime."

My uncle's hand dropped from his face. "So quick to take offense. Just like your mother."

Hal's shoulders hunched as he dug his hands into his pockets. "I don't think she'd appreciate the comparison."

"No," my uncle conceded wearily. "But I don't suppose you do either."

"What are you doing here?"

My uncle's response was so quiet, I didn't hear it.

Hal said, "I know the feeling."

He held the door open for his father and the two men went inside, thwarting further eavesdropping.

I stood at the open window, inhaling the wet yard smell, listening to water drip from the eaves to the porch.

Hal handicapped.

I remembered the Purple Heart, the Thorazine in his duffel bag. It must be bad, must be serious, for my uncle to be so affected. And yet, I'd have thought my uncle would be almost glad to discover a physical excuse for my cousin's poverty and antisocial behavior.

I'd have given anything to know what afflicted my quirky cousin; given anything to hear the rest of his conversation with my Uncle Henry.

And it occurred to me that maybe I could—by proxy. I'd left Sandy standing in the hall near the telephone—a perfect spot from which to eavesdrop.

There was a phone in my room, on the floor beneath the window (I hadn't leased quite enough furniture to fill the rooms). I picked up the receiver, meaning to break in on Sandy's call and ask him to keep his ears open.

But the voice on the telephone line rendered me mute.

It was a quiet voice, with a trace of a German accent. It was saying, "And what will Laura do about—"

If I hadn't known he was dead, I'd have sworn I was listening to Lennart Strindberg.

Sandy's voice cut in. "Someone's on the other line. Hello? Who's there?"

I was too shaken to announce myself. I hung up.

It had been fourteen years since I'd talked to Lennart Strindberg. I couldn't have described his voice after so long. But hearing the man on the phone, whoever he was, brought it back: the romantic, defeated quality, the faint, melodic accent.

I heard footsteps on the stairs, running steps: Sandy. And I realized I didn't want to know who he'd been talking to. I don't know why I reacted that way; maybe I was afraid I'd find out it was Lennart, maybe I was afraid I'd find out it wasn't.

I bent and unclipped the module that plugged the telephone wire into the wall. The footsteps were on the landing now, fast approaching my door.

I did the expedient thing. I set the phone outside on the windowsill, and quietly closed the window.

I was still standing by the window when Sandy came in without knocking.

I didn't want him coming closer to the window, so I

approached him. I met him in the middle of the room, at the foot of the bed. I knew I should embrace him; I knew that would be normal. I just stood there.

"Something's wrong," he observed.

"I heard my Uncle Henry come in."

Sandy nodded. "He's in the kitchen with Hal." His voice hardened as he said the name. "Your uncle's already had a snootful, and they're into your whiskey. Which reminds me," he added disingenuously, "the hall phone's not very private. Is there an extension somewhere?"

I shook my head. "I don't think so. I didn't order one."

Sandy glanced around the room. He noticed the telephone module under the window.

"Not in here," I lied. "I don't like being disturbed while I sleep."

Sandy smiled. "I've noticed."

Someone leaned on the doorbell—a jarring, grating sound.

"Reporters! Will you disable the bell for me, Sandy?"

He was saying, "Sure thing," when the buzzing turned into thumping and shouts so loud they could be heard all the way upstairs. Reporters don't usually shout and pound at doors; something was up.

Hal's voice rose above the din. "What the hell do you want?"

I heard a muffled reply, then there was a pause, and the sound of footsteps on the stairs again.

Hal appeared at my bedroom door. He looked at me and Sandy standing beside the bed, and his mouth set into its usual cynical line. "Cops at the door, my dear," he informed me. "Saying they've got a warrant to search the place."

I preceded Hal through the door and down the steps.

And sure enough, two plainclothesmen and two uniformed officers stood on the porch, causing a brouhaha among the reporters. I hustled the cops inside and closed the door on the reporters' shouts of, "Is this an arrest? What are you searching for? Will you cooperate, Miss Di—"

I recognized one of the plainclothesmen from my visit to the Lucky Logger that morning. One of the uniformed officers also looked vaguely familiar.

I said to the plainclothesman, "Show me the warrant."

He handed me the inexpertly typed document. It was signed by a magistrate I'd met the day before, at my office-warming party. It authorized the police to search my house "for weapons, especially but not necessarily limited to, handguns of the .22 and the .38 caliber variety; and written material of, by, or to Kirsten Strindberg; and evidence relating to the presence of Wallace Bean on the day of . . ."

"This part about evidence relating to the presence of Wallace Bean"—I waved the warrant—"it's unconstitutionally vague. The Fourth Amendment prohibits this kind of fishing expedition, where you look for anything that might be evidence of crime. And this stuff about searching for weapons 'not necessarily limited to'—that's just fishing, too. So, gentlemen, I put you on notice that I recognize your authority to search only for Kirsten Strindberg's letters, and for the handguns. And I don't recognize the existence of probable cause to search for those items, either. But that's something properly challenged in court."

The plainclothesmen exchanged give-me-a-break glances, and one of the two uniformed cops, the one who looked vaguely familiar, grinned as appreciatively as if I'd been a circus sideshow.

My Uncle Henry chose that moment to come in from the kitchen, looking a bit pink of eye and holding a tumbler of whiskey. He stopped short when he saw the cluster of men in my hallway.

"Dick! What's going on here?" Years of governance had imbued his voice with authority.

Dick, the cop from the Lucky Logger, shrugged his shoulders and tugged at his collar. "Well, Mayor, we were asked to execute this search warrant."

My uncle snatched the duplicate warrant out of the plainclothesman's hand. He skimmed it quickly, then tapped the signature. "Looks like the magistrate is still p.o.ed I took the Elks presidency away from him."

The plainclothesman stifled a hoot of laughter. "All I know is the captain told me to execute—"

"I'd like to execute the cap—"

"Uncle Henry!" I warned. It's not good policy to utter threats against police captains when their menials are present.

My uncle looked at me, swayed a little on his feet, then burst out laughing. "Every drunk old fart should have a lawyer in the family, eh, Dick?"

I decided I'd better get the mayor out of there until he sobered up a bit. "We'll be waiting in the backyard," I told the cops. I expected them to stop us, to frisk us and keep us under guard while they searched the house. It said a lot for my Uncle Henry that they didn't.

I took my uncle's arm and drew him toward the back of the house. He was definitely tanked, and he kept stopping to pat my hand.

"You turned out good, Laura. I always thought that mouth of yours would get you into trouble, and here you go and turn it into a gold mine."

We were almost out the back door when I began to wonder where Sandy was. Odd that he hadn't come down to see what the shouting was about.

When we got outside, I peered up at my bedroom window. I could see a blue uniform near the window. But no sign of Sander Arkelett.

Hal stepped up behind me. "Looking for your boyfriend?"

"He's not my—" I realized that he was. "He must still be upstairs."

Hal shook his head. "Not unless he came back inside."

"*Back* inside?"

"He climbed out your bedroom window. I saw him start out before I followed you downstairs." My cousin sounded pleased. "In fact, unless my night vision deceives me, your boyfriend pretty well demolished those geraniums."

Hal walked over the a mashed bush beside the back porch. "What the—?" He bent down and picked up a squarish object.

"What is it? What do you have?" My Uncle Henry sounded apprehensive.

Hal held up the object. "A telephone."

I glanced up at the windowsill. Sure enough, Sandy had knocked the telephone down when he made his departure. I wondered whether he'd seen it before he sent it toppling into the shrubbery.

I took the phone out of Hal's hands and put it on the porch. "I believe in talking to my flowers, Hal."

Hal stood up, looking from the bushes to the window above. "If you'd been listening in on someone's phone calls, and you didn't want him to know it was you on the extension, I guess the smart thing would be to unplug your phone and throw it out the window."

My uncle murmured something about how the phone company makes you pay to repair your phone if it thinks you've been careless with it.

In the light from the kitchen window, I could see Hal grinning down at me. He looked young and happy, the way he'd looked as a kid, tagging me in kick-the-can.

Seeing him that way stirred up a lot of feelings that definitely were *not* the smart thing.

22

My house was a disaster. All the unpacking I'd paid three movers fourteen dollars an hour apiece to do, the cops had undone in a couple of hours.

My uncle and I stood in the kitchen surveying the damage. Hal scrutinized me.

"I'm not going to burst into tears, if that's what you're wondering," I snapped, pushing damp hair off my face.

"I didn't think you were, Mowgli. But tell me, what would it take to make you cry?"

"A court order." I kicked aside what had formerly been the contents of my kitchen drawers.

Uncle Henry was growing indignant. "They can't do this to a *lawyer*! You sue them, Laura. Teach them a lesson."

"Have some more whiskey, Uncle Henry."

Hal found the bottle and handed it to his father. We left him sitting at the kitchen table while we went to survey the damage in the rest of the house.

At least, that's where I thought we were going.

Once we'd closed the kitchen door behind us, Hal grabbed my wrist and tugged me toward the front door.

"What are you doing?" I looked around the living room, at the heaps of cushions the police had pulled off the couch and chairs, at the drawers they'd pulled out of the hutch and desk, at the felt bottoms they'd torn off the lamps.

"We're going to the airport," Hal informed me.

I wasn't sure I'd heard him right. My mind was too much on the mess. I tried to jerk free, but he pulled me across the room and into the hall. He yanked my handbag off the banister, "Car keys in here?"

"Hey!" I protested, examining the delicate strap for damage.

Hal opened the front door, pushing me through the yammering wall of reporters. I paused long enough to tell them, no, I didn't know what the police had expected to find in my house, but no, they hadn't found it, whatever it was. The aspiring weather girl asked, "I don't suppose you'd let us in for a quick peek?" I told her she didn't suppose right. I looked around for Judy Britt, but she wasn't there. Probably home cooking dinner for a fat, reactionary husband.

I ended up driving myself and Hal to the airport, without a clue why we were going there. Hal would only say, "I want to talk to someone."

That someone turned out to be the girl at the rental car concession, the one who'd bestowed the dazzling smile on Sandy Arkelett that morning. She was locking up for the night. The evening flight had come and gone, and the airport was deserted, except for a young janitor wearing headphones and crooning "Oooo, baby" under his breath.

The girl, a chubby, short-waisted blonde, told us the airport was closed. Then she took a good look at us. Her jaw sagged and she shook her head.

Hal's voice was soothing. "You remember us from this morning, don't you? We came to pick up our friend."

"I hope I didn't get him in trouble," the girl blurted out. "I felt like I had to answer the policeman's questions." She leaned back, as though flinching from us.

Hal shook his head. "No, it's okay. You did the right thing. He'd not mad at you, not at all."

The girl looked relieved. "He isn't? Because I didn't mean to get him into trouble, but I felt like—"

"I know." Hal leaned across the counter. "But listen, can you tell us exactly what happened?"

"This man came, a policeman, you know, wearing a regular suit." She added defensively, "I made him show me his badge, though, before I'd—"

"Do you remember the policeman's name?"

The blonde shook her head. "Gee, I don't know. I was kind of shook up, but I don't think he ever said. He was older, with gray hair. Older than you," she added, as though that were scarcely possible.

"What did he ask you?"

"He asked me about one of our cars, the black Mustang. He wanted to know who had it last night."

Hal brushed eraser dust off the counter. "So you looked it up for him?"

"I didn't have to." She blushed, looking down at her vermilion nails. "I mean, I remembered. I didn't get him into any trouble, though? You're sure? 'Cause he seemed really nice."

My cousin smirked with self-satisfaction all the way back to the car.

I waited until we'd climbed in before further gratifying his ego. "Okay, how did you know?"

"The way she smiled at him this morning. This isn't the big city; girls here don't usually smile that way at men they haven't met." He sounded like he thought it was a shame.

As I put the Mercedes into gear, he continued, "The interesting thing is, why were the cops asking about that car?"

"I suppose they check car rental places routinely, after a murder. To see what strangers were in town." As far as

I was concerned, the greater mystery was why my lover and colleague had sneaked into town a day early, then lied to me about it.

I did an effortless ninety on the flat stretch along the dunes.

"Tell me what you and Sandy are really here for, Laura."

"And you'll tell me why you take Thorazine?"

"I don't take it."

"What was it prescribed for?"

I glanced at my cousin. The green dashboard lights caught the harsh angles of his face, leaving his eyes in shadow. "None of your fucking business," he said quietly.

I downshifted. The silence was total and strained.

When we got back to my house, we found camera lights flooding the porch. A smartly dressed woman I didn't recognize gripped a microphone and gestured toward the door.

I pulled over half a block shy of my house, squinting at the logo on her microphone. "Christ. A D.C. station. I hate to abandon your father, but I'm not up for a coast-to-coast appearance. Not tonight."

"There's always my place."

"That icebox?" I pulled away and took us to the Trade Winds Motel. Call me sentimental.

23

I RECOGNIZED THE proprietor. He was the same fat, slippered man from whom I'd rented a room fourteen years earlier. That night, I'd done so timidly, fearing that my papa would find me before Lennart arrived. My papa had physically dragged me out of my senior prom because he'd seen couples kissing on the dance floor; I'd eloped with Gary Gleason because there had been no other way to date him. If my papa had discovered me waiting for a man at a motel— I'd begged the proprietor not to tell any "older men" I'd checked in; and he'd warned me not to "do business" in his motel.

Tonight, I calmly handed the fat man my Gold Card and told him I wanted his best room. I glanced out the glass door at my cousin's hulking silhouette. I was better at hiding my trepidation, these days. If not my affection.

"Gosh, my other customer's got the best view. But if you don't mind facing the road, I've got a real nice—"

"I don't mind facing the road." The "view" he referred to was of commercial fishing boats floating in black oil and fish guts.

It wasn't a bad room. It had what I needed: a double bed.

Hal frowned down at it, his hands stuffed into his pockets. "One bed?" There was a stubborn set to his mouth, a contentious gleam in his eye.

"Not in the mood, cousin?" I said lightly. "Now that my boyfriend's not at the door?"

His lips curled into a sour excuse for a smile. "Sandy put you in the mood, up there in your room?"

I pulled off my sweater. "I guess so."

A little color crept into his cheeks. But he kept his distance.

"You said you like your women easy, Hal. How much easier can it get?"

"You call yourself easy? You're the most snooping, secretive—"

"Do you really want your own bed?"

His eyes strayed from my face. And I knew I had him. At least for the night.

24

THE COLD WOKE me. It was light outside, just barely, and the fog from the bay had seeped through the motel walls, chilling the sheets. Hal was sprawled on his stomach, and showed no sign of waking.

I warmed up under a hot shower, turning the tiny bathroom into a steambath. I opened the bathroom window a crack, to let out a little steam, and I noticed that the parking lot behind the motel had a solitary car in it: a black Mustang.

I remembered the girl at the airport saying Sandy had rented a black Mustang; I didn't remember her saying he'd returned it.

I told myself it would be too great a coincidence, ending up at the same motel as Sandy. I told myself there must be dozens of black Mustangs in town.

And yet—I had mentioned the Trade Winds to Sandy myself. He'd tried to get records of the motel's phone calls for the night of Lennart's death, tried to trace the call I'd gotten there that night. He might easily have taken a room at the Trade Winds; he'd been there before and knew how to find it.

I looked down at the Mustang, and thought of my Mercedes, parked on the other side of the motel, not far from the office. Sandy would drive right by it on his way out to the street. And the last thing in the world I wanted was to have Sandy Arkelett spot my car and come looking for me. The last thing in the world I wanted was to have him walk in on me and Hal.

Hal was still asleep, and I dressed quickly. I was on my way out to move my car down the street when it occurred to me that Hal might wake up while I was gone. I didn't want him to misinterpret my absence.

I rummaged through the drawers until I found some motel stationery and a cheap pen. I wrote: *There's a black Mustang out back—you can see it from the bathroom window. I'm moving the Mercedes in case it's Sandy's. I don't want him to intrude.* Then I added, before I could reason myself out of it, *Hal, I've never felt this way about anyone before.* I stared at the sentence. It was true. And a hell of a shock.

I walked out to my car, tiny stipples of fog clinging to my sweater, my hair, my eyelashes. I drove the Mercedes down the block, to the parking lot of another motel.

I thought I'd solved the problem. It turned out I didn't know how big the problem was.

I pulled the keys out of the ignition and the damned things fell to the floor. I was groping along the mat for them when my fingers encountered something cold, protruding slightly from under the seat. I yanked on it, but it got hung up on the springs of the bucket seat. I slumped to see what it was.

There was no mistaking it: it was the barrel of a gun. I tugged until it came free.

It was a long-barreled revolver. It was Wallace Bean's gun, or one just like it. I left it on the mat and stared at it, feeling nauseous.

Two matched guns. One ended up at Kirsten Strindberg's house, and the other in my car. One of them had probably killed poor, stupid Wally. Which, I didn't know.

For the moment, I was more concerned with how the gun had found its way into my car.

Only three people had set foot in the Mercedes in the last two days: me, Hal, and Sandy.

Hal I eliminated because he'd never been in the car alone, that I knew of.

That left Sander Arkelett, who'd come to town a day early and lied to me about it; who'd arrived at Hal's house shortly after an armed intruder had left it; who'd been carrying a wet anorak not unlike the hooded affair the intruder had worn; who'd jumped out a second-story window to avoid meeting the police at my house.

I pushed the gun back under my seat, found my keys, and got out of the car. My first priority was to rouse Hal and get the hell away from the motel, away from that black Mustang.

I thought about Sandy as I walked back to the Trade Winds. I'd told him about Lennart Strindberg one night, when we'd been doing some serious drinking. Not long afterward, he claimed to be going to my hometown on a case. He offered to find out what had become of Lennart. I was surprised when he didn't stop at a few simple inquiries, when he went to the trouble of going through old obituaries.

He even looked up Lennart's will, even looked up the leases on the property described in the will, including the building that housed White, Sayres & Speck.

I thought he'd done it to impress me. But now—

My great plan—to return to my hometown and wreak havoc on Gary's and Kirsten's lives—began to look less my own, and more like something into which I'd been manipulated. I was beginning to think I'd been set up.

I was beginning to think Sandy Arkelett was a hell of a lot smarter than me, and a lot more dangerous.

I walked up the driveway of the Trade Winds, and there he was: driving toward me in the black Mustang.

Sandy looked surprised at first, then suspicious—a state I did not wish to encourage in him. Not until I figured out what he was up to.

Taking a determined breath, I strode up to the car. As he rolled down the window, I complained, "This is the third motel I've been to, looking for you!"

Sandy stroked his jaw thoughtfully. "Without your car?"

"My car's down the block at the last motel I tried. Where the hell were you last night? And where did you get this car?"

Sandy reached out and slipped his hand behind my neck, pulling me down for a kiss.

If Sandy Arkelett was a killer, I didn't want to find out the hard way. I kissed him back. "Why did you leave my house last night?"

"I don't much enjoy parties once the cops have crashed them." Sandy's smile crinkled the skin around his eyes. "I checked back later, but no one was around."

"I took my uncle home, and I stayed there a while.

After the cops left, the reporters were like sharks in bloody water!''

Sandy nodded. ''Yeah, I'll bet. I rented myself this car, and turned in here for a night's sleep.'' He reached across to the passenger side and unlocked the door. ''Get in.''

I walked around the back of the car, glancing at the room I'd shared with Hal. The curtains were still closed. I climbed into the Mustang.

But instead of driving out to the street, Sandy backed up and turned around, heading for the bay side of the motel.

''What are you doing?'' I managed to keep the alarm out of my voice.

He smiled dreamily. ''I've still got my key, and check-out time isn't until noon.''

''I've got a lot on my mind,'' I said firmly. ''And a hell of a mess to clean up at home.''

He stopped the car, rubbing his thumb over the galloping horse on the steering wheel. ''All right,'' he said quietly. ''I'll help you clean up.''

If I could have thought of an excuse to leave him, however preposterous, I'd have used it. But I couldn't. I said, ''Okay.''

25

I SPENT THE day barricaded inside my house with Sandy, putting things back into cupboards and drawers. We kept the curtains closed (cameras were poised like buzzards on the shoulders of reporters outside), so it was gloomy work. Vodka would have helped, but I was too leery of my companion to risk dulling my wits.

It was nearly evening when my Aunt Diana phoned to ask me what I was wearing to the "fête."

"Oh, no!" I'd forgotten about her damned party. "I can't come! I'd seem heartless, going to a party the day after my client gets killed. Plus Kirsten, who used to be a friend of mine."

I could hear the irritation in her short, controlled breaths. "This party is in *your* honor!" my aunt reminded me. "The arrangements have been made for *weeks*."

Weeks ago, a party at the Mayor's Residence had seemed an excellent way to ally myself with the pillars of society Gary Gleason had alienated over the years—the ones who Kiwanised and Elked with superior court judges. But now—

A voice in my head said, *Do it anyway. Pull his damned career out from under him.*

My aunt began a shrill recital of the trouble she'd taken on my account. She'd been trying to acquire me for one of her parties ever since I'd made national news representing Bean; she had no intention of letting me wriggle off the hook now.

I held the receiver away from my ear. I had wanted to tear Gary away from Kirsten as painfully as possible; and that end had been achieved, though not according to my plan. Since I had no intention of becoming a small town public defender, the game was over. So why did I still want to score off Gary Gleason?

"All right," I interrupted my aunt. "All right, I'll come."

Kirsten was dead, and someone had tried to kill Gleason. But that didn't necessarily absolve them of Lennart's murder. Maybe, in some way I didn't understand, it even proved they'd done it. There was no harm in making Gleason squirm a while longer. God knows, he'd made *me*—

I hung up quickly. What I did, I did for Lennart Strindberg. Not for me. Jesus. Not for *me*.

Sandy whispered in my ear, "Sit down, honey. You look a little shook up."

I hadn't heard him come up behind me. My shoulders knotted when he touched his lips to my neck. Afraid of my friends, unsure of my enemies—

I wheeled around, pushing him away. "Damn that shallow, stupid woman!" I spat. "I hate my aunt! I've always hated her! She used to go around telling people she'd taken my mother's place! Saying what a big responsibility it was! Which meant she came over twice a week with a bakery coffee cake! And she didn't like me to play with Hal when we were kids. You know why? She wanted him to play with the hotshot boys, the doctors' sons. To be a big macho sports hero. Which he was, for a while." And I'd only just stopped disliking him for it. "She even bought him a red Fiat Spider when he was sixteen! Had a *reporter* come over and take pictures of Uncle Henry handing him the keys! That's when it finally got to Hal! He used to leave the car in the driveway and walk everywhere. Did you know he turned down Princeton to go to the local junior college? That's why he didn't get a student deferment!''

"An embarrassment of riches?" Sandy blinked his sleepy eyes at me. "Wish I'd had that problem!"

I started up the stairs.

"What time are we going to the party?" he asked gently.

We. I stared down at him. "Did I mention it to you?"

He nodded. "You told me to bring a tux." He looked disconcertingly relaxed. Familiar. The same as ever.

I wanted to ask him why he'd come to town a day early. Why he'd lied about it. Who he'd been talking to on the phone last night. But I remembered his dripping anorak, his thirty-eight caliber Detective Special: two things in common with the man who'd shot at me.

And the first rule of cross-examination is: *Don't ask a question unless you already know the answer.* I couldn't risk a wrong answer. Not when we were alone.

"You don't have to come," I suggested cautiously.

Sandy pushed a pale cascade of hair off his forehead and shrugged. "Shame to waste the tux."

I visualized the soft leather suitcase he'd carried out of the airport. He certainly hadn't packed a tuxedo in there. Was he trying to maneuver me into asking if he'd flown in early, with baggage I hadn't seen? Trying to smoke an accusation out of me; trying to find out how much I already knew?

"Okay," I said, turning away.

I went upstairs and locked my bedroom door. I heard Sandy go out. I took a shower and put on my green silk dress.

When I went back downstairs, Sandy was in black tie, straightening his cummerbund. He looked me over. "My favorite dress," he commented appreciatively.

And I answered truthfully. "That's why I brought it."

It took us a few minutes to get to my car. The crowd of reporters had thinned, but the few who persisted (none of the San Francisco crowd; just local stations and a couple from Oregon) insisted on getting some dull footage of my scowling face. They filmed the Mercedes pulling away from the curb.

"Turn the corner here, would you, Laura? I want to get my car. Case I decide to leave early."

I followed Sandy's directions to the Mustang, wondering why he'd parked so far from my house. Wondering if it had anything to do with the policeman who'd inquired about it at the airport.

Sandy followed me to my aunt and uncle's house, so I didn't have a chance to do anything about the gun that was (I assumed) still jammed into the springs under my seat. I'd have to ditch the damned thing as soon as I could. Somewhere safe, this time.

I slid into a parking place near the mayor's fake chalet, and let Sandy go scout out his own parking place.

The porch was flooded with light from mock sconces on either side of the double door, and every lamp in the house was burning, spilling light into the redwoods and rhododendrons flanking the house. My car was in a pocket of darkness between the house and the street lamp across the street. I could hear car doors slamming, up and down the block.

Middle-aged couples, most of them stuffed into unstylish dress clothes, walked past me on their way to the party, the women trying to protect their hairdos from the wind.

Discreetly parked in front of the house was the unmarked police car in which I'd traveled to the Lucky Logger the morning before.

I watched Sandy saunter toward my car. The tuxedo was perfect on his long, lean body, and black flattered his sand-colored hair and pale skin.

I climbed out of the car and reluctantly took his arm. He fastened his hand over mine.

On the walkway we encountered Judy Britt, looking better than usual in navy crepe. "Laura! You came!"

I always assume I'm on the record, when I talk to a reporter. "Nothing can bring back Kirsten Strindberg or Wallace Bean, so I put my feelings aside to honor a long-standing commitment." Pompous and empty—let her print it.

My papa came out to greet us. He bowed to Judy Britt and shook Sandy's hand, eyeing him coolly. Me, he drew inside to kiss, pet, and admire extravagantly. All the while, I worried about the dents and scratches I'd discovered on the bumper of his Lincoln.

My aunt looked disdainfully at my gown and said, "A fitted bodice—what an old-fashioned touch." She wore a sparkly paisley tube of a dress with a short chiffon cape that made her look like she was about to get her hair done.

I introduced her to Sandy, and her smile went from forced to flirtatious. She stood a trifle too close to him, and began asking him questions. I heard Sandy tell her that he was a computer operator, that he'd come to town to install my computer system. My aunt laughed as though she thought nothing could be more charming and amusing than installing computer systems.

I looked around the high-ceilinged room. My aunt had moved her furniture (the city's furniture, I should say) to accommodate a crowd, and she'd stocked gold-clothed tables with ice chests, bottles, and glasses for mix-it-yourself bars. There were thirty or forty people in the room already. Middle- and retirement-aged couples, mostly. A few people my age; some with familiar faces—inevitable in a town with only one high school. Several guests had noted my entrance, and I smiled vaguely at them. Junior college students *cum* caterers passed through the crowd with trays of hors d'oeuvres.

I spotted Hal across the room, leaning against the wall, staring at me. He wore a dark suit that had probably fit him once; now it was tight across the chest, loose at the waist.

I'd expected him to phone me after he found my note. Schoolgirlish of me, I supposed.

He straightened slowly, standing away from the wall. His eyes glittered, and his half smile was contemptuous. He turned away.

I abandoned Sandy to my aunt, and went to the nearest makeshift bar. I poured myself a vodka martini, without the vermouth. I stood alone, drinking it. A lot of people gawked; no one approached. Maybe the murders had left them tongue-tied; maybe it was my "celebrity." I doubted it would last long.

It didn't. A short, stout woman with a topknot and pointy glasses ("Mrs. Oriellini; you remember me, dear!") dug a veiny claw into my silk sleeve. "You were married to that boy who got run over day before yesterday, weren't you? I remember seeing your wedding picture in the paper. You had a short dress on, so I thought you must have eloped." She tilted her head inquiringly.

I smiled, trying to rotate my wrist out of her grasp. I ended up refilling my glass one-handed.

"Then I remember seeing in the paper in the legal notices that you got divorced from him." Mrs. Oriellini squinted, tapping her orange mouth with a dinner-ringed finger. "And there was that business about your car, too."

"My car?" I wished my aunt had invested a few bucks in decent vodka.

Mrs. Oriellini leaned toward me, slopping part of her cocktail onto the carpet. "That boy who got gassed because of the policeman's son."

I was beginning to feel the first martini. "I'm sorry, I don't know what you mean."

"Sure you do, honey. His name was Hamburg, or

Frankfurt, something like that. No, no, Strongberg—that's it. Leonard Strongberg." She nodded, her stiffly sprayed topknot bobbing.

"I wasn't here then." I yanked my arm away. "Please excuse me, I should—"

"Oh, well," she commiserated. "I guess you didn't want your car back after that."

"No." I turned to leave.

"Even if you went and got it repaired, you'd worry it would do that again."

She had me, damn her. I turned back. "Do what?"

"Leak that gas. Carbon dioxide."

"Monoxide," I corrected automatically. "But I heard—" I couldn't bring myself to say his name, "I heard that he ran a hose from the muffler into the car."

The woman's eyes sparkled and her double chin became pronounced as she tucked her head down and whispered, "Well, *someone* did. But they found that crack under the car—in the manifest, I think it's called—it was letting poison carbon gas right in through the heater. Didn't you know?"

"It's been so long. Wasn't there some trouble about it, afterward?"

"Well, there certainly should have been! But being as he was a policeman's boy, they dropped the whole thing! Let him go sign up for the army."

I felt my fingers sink into her soft flesh of her arm. "When you say 'someone' ran a hose from the muffler—"

"The policeman, if you ask me!" Her tone was thrilled and confidential. "That boy of his had got in trouble for the very same thing a few months before that. No one got hurt that time, but the gas made the poor lady fall asleep and run right off the road. Lucky it happened near the dunes—if she'd been up in the redwoods—" Mrs. Oriellini shook her head darkly.

I dropped the old gossip's arm and stepped back, colliding with a wizened gynecologist who had a reputation for letting his buddies know if their daughters weren't virgins. I'd had a screaming fit when my aunt suggested Papa send me to him for "a checkup." Now, I had some kind of conversation with him; about San Francisco restaurants, I think. I also met his wife. She wanted to know if I'd ever heard of an L.A. lawyer who was suing them.

A crowd began to gather around me and I clicked into automatic pilot, shaking hands, hearing modest success stories from schoolmates I didn't remember, assuring family friends that I found the "Old Town" renovation charming.

But I was thinking about Captain Loftus. When I'd met him, I'd recognized the surname. He'd mentioned his son John, but that didn't account for it—I hadn't thought of John in years. No, I remembered now that I'd run across the name in a newspaper article accompanying Lennart's obituary. Something about "Police Sergeant Emmanuel Loftus" discovering Lennart's body.

I noticed Mrs. Oriellini standing with Hillsdale High's ancient and fascistic principal. She winked a shrewd, myopic eye at me.

If Lennart Strindberg had been parked near the jetty in the Volkswagen—waiting to meet someone, perhaps?—he'd certainly have kept the engine running and the car heater on. It was freezing cold out there, always.

Maybe Captain Loftus (Sergeant Loftus, then) had happened upon Lennart, dead from exhaust fumes pumped in through the heater. His son John had recently repaired the Volkswagen; maybe the sergeant had known that. Maybe he'd worried that history had repeated itself, that his son had again failed to spot a deadly crack in the exhaust manifold. Maybe the sergeant had run a length of hose from the tailpipe to the front window. That way, even if the police did examine the car and find the leak, they wouldn't attribute Lennart's death to it. Not when there was evidence Lennart had killed himself.

Maybe Loftus had forced his son into the army to squelch inquiry into the inadequate car repair. If so, he'd done John no favor. It's a short jail sentence for involuntary manslaughter; Vietnam had been a death sentence.

But one thing still rankled. How the hell had Lennart managed to drive my car all the way out to the jetty?

And if he'd been sitting there running the car heater, for whom had he been waiting?

The possibility that occurred to me was chilling, it was so damned cold-blooded.

26

MY AUNT HAD buttonholed Sandy again. She made fluttery gestures with her hands and looked at him in a bright, party sort of way, blithering endlessly. Sandy bent closer to listen, one hand in his pocket and the other holding a drink. He smiled halfheartedly.

As often as we'd talked about Lennart's death, Sandy had never mentioned a police examination of the VW; he'd never mentioned a carbon monoxide leak in the exhaust system. Was it something even a good detective might not discover, fourteen years after the fact? Or just one more thing Sander Arkelett had chosen not to tell me?

I'd poured out my whole tale of woe to him; reopened

all the wounds. I'd allied myself with him, strategically, emotionally, and physically. What the hell was he playing at?

A voice beside me murmured, "He's a big hit with my mother."

"Hal!" I blinked myself back to here-and-now. "Nice of you to say hello."

"You make a terrific couple," he continued. "Sophisticated, elegant." He watched Sandy shake a green olive out of his glass and into his mouth. "I suppose he explained why he flew into town a day early?"

"I didn't ask."

A flicker of a frown disturbed my cousin's impassivity. "You trust him," he concluded.

I couldn't keep the bitterness out of my voice. "*You* do, apparently."

"Meaning what?"

"You saw my note, didn't you?"

He hesitated, then admitted, "I saw it."

My aunt glanced our way. "Henry!" she called, irritation bristling in her tone. She slipped her arm through Sandy's, obliging him to escort her to our corner of the room. "You might exert yourself to mingle a little bit, instead of standing here bothering Laura!"

Hal did not kiss the cheek his mother offered.

Her lips pursed crossly. Then she laughed her artificial laugh. "I suppose the local boys seem quite dull compared to *your* friends, eh, Laura?" She winked coquettishly at Sandy.

Sandy casually draped his free arm around my shoulder. He nodded to Hal. "Good to see you again."

My aunt yanked Hal's lapel; it didn't make his suit fit any better. "You've met my son?"

"Sure," Sandy smiled. "We were out at Hal's place yesterday."

My aunt's penciled-on brows failed to disguise a frown

that would have looked much like Hal's if nature had been allowed to take its course. She observed to Sandy, "*This* is Henry's home, of course." She emphasized the name Henry. "And a lot of trouble he'd save the city, too, if he'd stop this camping-out nonsense!"

Hal's mouth pinched into an angry line.

But my aunt did not let up. "The police have to send a patrol car out there two or three times a day to make sure he hasn't started a fire with his lanterns! The only reason they don't kick him right out of there like they would anyone else is that he's *our* son." Her voice was rich with irony as she admitted the relationship.

Hal took a step backward, looking as though he'd just seen something loathsome. Then he shook his head and turned away. I watched him thread his way through the crowd, ignoring latecomers' attempts to greet him as he escaped through the front door.

Sandy broke the uncomfortable silence. "Where's Mayor Di Palma tonight, ma'am? I've been wanting to pay my respects."

If Sandy meant to reduce tensions, he'd taken the wrong approach. My aunt flushed, her head trembling on its short neck. "He's ill," she said brusquely. "If you'll excuse me, I *must* speak to the caterer."

We watched her stalk into the dining room.

"One big happy family," Sandy said dryly. Then he added, "No offense!"

"I've had it, Sandy! I'm leaving!"

Two mink-stoled matrons on our right glowered their disapproval. I heard one whisper, "Too good for us now!"

I set what remained of my drink onto a gilded occasional table, purposely ignoring the coaster. When I looked up, Emmanuel Loftus was approaching. Where the hell had he come from?

Sandy's arm slipped from my shoulder. By the time the captain greeted me, Sandy was halfway to the dining room.

"You're looking very pretty tonight, Miss Di Palma."
The captain ran a finger under his starched collar. "Often
as I wear these monkey suits, always wish I was off duck-
hunting, instead." Say what he might, there was no sug-
gestion of the hick about him. He presented a trim and
very tidy figure in navy wool and a red silk tie. "I think
it's fine you took the trouble to come—all things considered. It's the kind of gesture means a lot to a person's
family."

Family. I supposed a good father would manufacture
evidence to keep his son out of trouble. I'd smashed up
my bumper to protect my papa.

"Can I get you another drink, Miss Di Palma? Sometimes all this fatted-calf stuff—it kinda makes you remember why you went away in the first place."

Apparently Loftus had observed our family conference.

I let him bring me another drink. Straight vodka. Something else he'd observed, in the course of the evening.

"Is this business or pleasure for you, Captain?"

He ran a hand over the back of his silver waves, grinning sheepishly. "Well, I *was* invited."

"But that's not the main reason you're here? Are you
keeping an eye on me?" I took a quick gulp of my drink.
No use sipping cheap vodka.

"I wouldn't put it like that." The captain's face crinkled
with concern. "You're a pro, Miss Di Palma. As good as
they get at what you do, I guess. Well—" He shrugged.
"I like to think I am, too—even if Hillsdale is a smallish
sort of place to do it in. So I won't lie to you. Sure I'm
interested in you. And your friend." He gestured toward
the dining room, into which Sandy had just vanished. "But
I'm not keeping tabs on you or anything like that. More
just getting a feeling for you, if you understand me."

"So now you know I'm not particularly fond of my
aunt." I held up my drink. "And that I like this stuff
straight up."

He smiled apologetically. "I guess I know a little more than that."

"Such as?" So much for the first rule of cross-examination.

"Well," his smile was avuncular, "I'd say that tall fellow"—again he gestured toward the dining room—"better keep an eye on your cousin."

I assumed—then, at least—that he meant romantically.

We were interrupted by a chipper brunette who bubbled over with "big plans" for the next reunion of our high school class. I listened, hoping I wouldn't be around long enough to attend. Captain Loftus excused himself somewhere between the name tags with yearbook pictures on them and the testimonial plaque for our beloved English teacher.

It took me five or ten minutes to escape the woman's cloying enthusiasm. I made my way past the dining room buffet (no sign of Sandy), and slipped out the kitchen door.

I stood on the redwood deck inhaling cold wind, and watching planters of fuchsia swing on their wire hangers. What if Mrs. Oriellini was right? Captain Loftus was certainly clever enough to recognize a situation that might ruin his son. He was also clever—and fatherly—enough to do something about it.

I rubbed my arms to warm them; the silk felt like slick ice.

If Loftus had run that hose from the VW's exhaust pipe to the front window, it definitely complicated matters. But I wasn't sure it changed anything.

I tiptoed through the well-lit side yard, trying to keep my four-inch heels from sinking into the damp lawn.

I thought I heard someone or something moving through the tall rhododendrons separating the yard from the gully beside it.

"Hal?" I called out quietly.

The rustling ceased; no one answered.

I looked around the yard; no one there but me. Me and the fluttering shadows of potted fuchsias. I felt a chill of apprehension. I tried again, with more authority in my voice. "Who's there?"

Then I heard twigs snapping and the sucking sound of footsteps in the mud. They seemed to be coming from the gully.

There were too damned many people prowling around. I dashed across the lawn to my car.

I turned the key in the lock and was surprised to find myself locking, rather than locking, the door. I knew I hadn't left the Mercedes open. Not with that gun under my seat.

I climbed into the car, feeling under the seat for the revolver. I groped around for a full two minutes, breaking a couple of nails and pinching my fingers in the springs.

The damned gun had disappeared. Again!

27

MY AUNT STOOD on the porch offering her cheek to departing guests. I sat in the Mercedes, watching absent-mindedly. She kept glancing over her shoulder into the vestibule, apparently looking for someone. My papa probably; he seemed to be ersatz host of the fête. I wondered vaguely what had become of him; I hadn't seen him since he'd first greeted me.

Less vaguely, I wondered who the hell had taken the Buntline Scout out of my car. Sandy knew how to pick locks. And he'd had time to do some burgling, while I chatted with Captain Loftus and the high school reunion organizer. But why would he want a twenty-two? He had his own gun.

I put the car into gear. If Sander Arkelett had the twenty-two, it meant he didn't want to use his own gun. But use it for what? On whom?

I laid scratch, pulling away from the curb. I suddenly wanted to be far away, fast. Away from Sandy, away from my vituperative aunt, away from the folksily perspicacious captain, and most of all, away from my cavalier cousin.

The note I'd left Hal at the motel—it must have occurred to him when he read it—when I didn't come back—that I'd run into Sandy outside. And though Hal had gone to some trouble to make me distrust Sandy, he hadn't bothered to phone me and satisfy himself that I'd escaped the encounter unscathed.

Besides which, we'd spent a hell of a terrific night together. And not so much as a "Thank you, ma'am."

I squealed around the nearest corner, down a long stretch of side street flanking the gully beside my aunt's house. I was starting to floor it when my headlights slid over a car parked in a curbside river of rainwater. Sandy's Mustang.

It was the only car around. The street had gully on either side; no houses, no street lamps. Just one black car.

I pulled up alongside it. Shifted into park and climbed out of the Mercedes. Peered into the Mustang's dark interior. No one inside.

If Sandy *had* taken the twenty-two, chances were he'd stashed it in his rented car. The damned gun was two feet long; not easily tucked into a cummerbund.

I hesitated, hand on the driver's window. Sandy had once shown me how to slip a wire under a car window and pull up the lock. I knew I had a coat hanger in the Mercedes. The question was whether I *wanted* to find the revolver—and what the hell I'd do with it if I did find it.

I'd keep it away from Sandy. I could do that much.

I was getting the hanger out of my trunk when I heard shots. Two of them, less than a second apart, no louder than firecrackers but deeper in pitch. They came from the gully or from my aunt's rhododendrons beyond it.

A sudden blast of wind brought up the decayed smell of skunk cabbage. I stood there for a minute, coat hanger dangling from my fingers. Wind flayed my face, my skirt flapped, goose bumps rose on my arms and legs. I tried to believe I'd heard cars backfiring. Cherry bombs. I dropped the hanger and climbed back into the Mercedes.

I made myself turn around and go back to my aunt's house. My high heels wouldn't get me through the oozing mud of the gully, but I could check the rhododendron bushes.

I didn't want to admit it to myself, but I was harboring the morbid fear that Sander Arkelett had just shot my cousin.

What I found was equally distressing.

Light from my aunt's deck and side yard filtered through the thick hedge, faintly illuminating the shadowy, storm-tossed tangle of vegetation beyond. On the margin of relatively dry ground between the rhododendrons and the sloping gully, I found Sandy Arkelett.

He was slumped against a skinny redwood tree. One leg was buckled beneath him and the other extended straight out in front. Pale light glinted in his hair, and I could see that his head lolled. A white spot against the black of his suit jacket appeared to be his own hand, clamped over his heart. And, dark against the grayed whiteness of his shirt, a stain spread upward toward his collar.

I felt my high heels sink into the soft dirt. My knees sank too; I felt cold, leaf-strewn mud on my legs. I felt my fingers knot themselves into my hair, and I heard myself make a sound. Not a moan, not a scream; somewhere in between.

Almost immediately, Emmanuel Loftus was on his knees beside me, pressing my face to his chest, shouting to somebody. His voice rumbled unintelligibly behind the crisp warmth of his shirt.

And I never got a chance to go to Sandy. Two plainclothes cops beat through the bushes, swearing and snapping branches, and the captain turned me over to one of them, ordering, "Get her inside! And keep everyone away from her! And for pity's sake, warm her up!"

As one of the policeman dragged me, almost literally dragged me, away, I managed a backward glance at Sandy.

The captain and the other officer knelt over him, pulling his hand away from his chest.

28

I SLUMPED ON MY father's bed. The plainclothesman who'd searched my house the evening before threw a bedspread around my shoulders. I shrugged it off.

Sandy shot. Did it mean I'd been right to suspect him of God knows what? Or did it prove him innocent?

Maybe it didn't matter. Maybe all that mattered was that

I'd made love to him (if not loved him) for most of a long, bitter winter. And now he might be dying. Might be dead.

I was too shocked to cry. I heard my father pounding on his bedroom door, asking what was the matter. The cop said, "Sorry, sir, police business. I can't let you see Miss Di Palma until the captain says so." My aunt responded with an outraged, "This is *my* house, you know!"

Who could have shot Sandy? Why?

Why specifically, I didn't know. But I knew it must involve my plan to hurt Gary Gleason, to hurt him the way he'd hurt me.

And I realized with sickening clarity that it *was* me—my own pain—I'd wanted to avenge; not Lennart's death, not really. Hal was right—I hadn't loved Lennart Strindberg; I had merely saved face by thinking so.

My God, what kind of scheme had I set in motion, that people should end up—

"Is he dead?" I asked the plainclothesman for the twentieth time.

The man fidgeted with something in his pocket, peering out my father's bedroom window at the redwood deck below. "I didn't get a good look," he repeated.

It was about an hour before Captain Loftus tapped at the door. I heard his pleasant Oklahoma drawl as he assured my father, "You can see her in just a minute, Mr. Di Palma. I'll have Dick fetch you when we're done."

Then he slipped through the door, shutting it tight behind him. His navy blue suit was streaked with mud, a bit of crumbled leaf adhered to his hair, and he rubbed his hand with a linen handkerchief. "Shot twice in the chest," he said immediately. "But it could've been worse. Paramedics don't think it touched the heart. Probably some damage to the lungs. Too early to say." He squatted beside the bed, squinting sympathetically.

"He's not dead?"

"No. Definitely not dead." The captain put his arms around me and I broke down.

I heard the plainclothes cop shuffle nervously around the room, and I pulled myself together. "Did he say anything? Did he say who shot him?"

The captain murmured, "Talked a little. Which is a good sign. He's not choking—good sign for the lungs."

I gripped Loftus's lapels. "What did he say?"

"That it was too dark to see who shot him."

"Did *you* see anyone out there?"

He shook his head. "But we're still looking. We'll find something, don't worry. You should try and get a little sleep, maybe."

"Sleep! My God! I've got to get over to the hospital!"

"I thought you might feel that way. Dick, take her over to County, will you?" He gave me a gentle shake. "I wouldn't want to see you driving tonight, Miss Di Palma."

It occurred to me, riding in Dick's unmarked car, that Captain Loftus hadn't asked me why I'd been out in the bushes soon after (and for all he knew, at the very moment) Sandy was shot.

I wondered why he hadn't.

29

SANDY WAS IN surgery when I got to the hospital. Five hours later, the nurse on duty told me they'd "closed him up" and taken him to intensive care. She said only immediate family was allowed in.

I spent the night on a padded bench in the hall. My papa came to the hospital to try to talk me into coming home. He sat with me for a while, but it made me uncomfortable having him there; I finally asked him to leave. I wanted to ask if he knew where Hal was. But I didn't; I was afraid he'd say police headquarters.

I was shambling back and forth along the corridor when the administrative nurse, the one whose name I'd seen on a door the day before, came looking for me. She brought me a cup of coffee, and said how nice to see me again after so many years. She said the doctors had removed two bullets from Sandy's chest. Neither bullet had touched his heart, and if he didn't develop pneumonia or a lung infection, he should pull through. The nurse, grown very fat over the years, seemed shocked when I inquired what caliber the bullets were. She said she didn't know. When I asked her to find out, she said maybe she'd better check with the police first.

Captain Loftus found me crumpling a Styrofoam cup.

"Captain!" I tossed the cup away. "What did you find? Do you know who shot him?"

He shook his head ruefully, sinking onto the bench beside me. His pant legs—he still wore the navy blue suit—were caked with mud, and there were dark circles under his eyes. "Didn't find much out there, I'm afraid. Pity your friend didn't see anything. I don't suppose *you* saw anything?"

"I wondered when you'd get around to asking."

There was a glint of irritation in his eyes.

I added hastily, "I assumed you had your reasons for waiting."

"I was curious what you were doing out there, of course. But I knew you weren't going anywhere." He frowned at his ruined shoes. "And I knew you'd have told me right away, anything that might have assisted our search."

Sensible, if unusually civil for a cop. "What caliber bullet—"

"Lab's got 'em. We'll know more in a while."

"But you must know what caliber—"

"What took you out to those bushes, Miss Di Palma?"

I considered asking about the bullets again. But I realized Loftus didn't mean to answer. "I'd just left my aunt's party, just turned the corner onto Clegg Street when I heard the shots. I turned around and went back. To take a look."

The captain raised his grizzled brows and blinked at me a few times. "Now that took some guts! With somebody out there shooting off a gun!"

"Guts? I don't know. I wasn't thinking. I was just afraid it might be . . . someone I cared about."

"Intuition? Well, you were certainly right."

"Yes." I saw no point in telling him it was Hal I'd been worried about, Sandy I'd mistrusted. "Practically the first thing I saw was Sandy. And then—"

"And then I found you."

"You heard the shots too?"

"Yuh. Went out and scouted around. Heard somebody in that bit of ravine, right before I come upon you." He rose wearily, stretching a little. With his suit jacket unbuttoned, I could see something dark under his arm. A shoulder holster. "I'll be back by in a while, Miss Di Palma. You think it over. Maybe something'll come back to you."

I watched him walk down the hall. San Francisco Homicide would have stuck me in a tiny room with soundproofed cork walls. One, maybe two teams of inspectors would have asked me for every detail: When exactly did I hear the shots? What did they sound like? What was I doing at the time? Why did I think someone had been shot? Why did I risk going back? Why didn't I call the cops? How long did it take me to get back? How long was I in the shrubbery? What exactly did I see and hear? Did Sandy speak to me? Had we been quarreling? Were we lovers?

I remembered the adage about the devil you know.

30

THAT EVENING, TWO nurses wheeled Sandy into Gary Gleason's old room. Gary, I learned, had checked out right after my visit.

I sneaked in behind the nurses, watching them position

the bed, plugging monitors into bits of plastic taped to Sandy's neck and abdomen. Sandy was newsprint white, in a drooling narcotic sleep, with tubes running into his nose and out from under the sheet on his chest. Plastic bags dangled from attachments to the bed, dripping something into his veins. Small, nozzled tanks of oxygen were arranged on his bedside table.

The nurses shooed me out of the room before I had a chance to get close.

I was as depressed as I could remember feeling, ever. I trudged to the padded bench, hardly noticing the man in the hall—until he wheeled around and strode rapidly toward the exit. Six feet four, maybe six five; longish white-blond hair; and most of all, the carriage.

"Lennart!" My gasp sounded a little hysterical.

The man stopped. His shoulders hunched. He turned around slowly. Reluctantly.

I blinked several times, expecting him to shimmer out of being right before my eyes. Lennart Strindberg. Unchanged. Lennart at twenty-one.

He said, "You are Laura Di Palma, are you not?"

The voice was like a punch in the stomach. I knew it couldn't be, knew it wasn't, and yet it looked like Lennart—and talked like him.

I opened my mouth. Couldn't speak. Ended up crying.

The boy's eyes glazed with tears, his pale cheeks grew pink. He ran a delicate hand through his corn silk hair.

"You're Dieter Strindberg. You must be." I brushed my tears away.

He nodded. "I am sorry to startle you in this way." He walked toward me, stopping just short of the padded bench.

From a distance of five feet, I could see the differences between the brothers. Lennart had been a little shorter, a little heavier. His cheekbones had been more pronounced, his chin stronger.

Dieter Strindberg said, with a trace of German accent, "I wish very much to see Mr. Arkelett. Is he—? He is not in danger of—?"

"If he doesn't get pneumonia, he'll probably make it."

The young man watched a nurse come out of Sandy's room with an armload of crumpled linen. His shoulders sagged. "I do not know, I am not sure what is the best thing for me to do now."

"You were talking to Sandy on the phone day before yesterday. Is he working for you?"

He nodded. "Yes, for three months now Sander is finding evidence that Lennart did not murder himself."

Three months. It had been less than three months since Sandy had asked me about my divorce, and (it now seemed) manipulated me into talking about Lennart. It had been less than three months since Sandy had volunteered to find out what had become of Lennart. It had been less than three months since Sandy had brought me the news of Lennart's suicide and Kirsten Strindberg's inheritance. It had been less than three months since Sandy had encouraged me to open an office in my hometown and blackmail an admission of guilt from Gary Gleason.

In fact, though I'd known him casually for more than a year, it had been less than three months since Sander Arkelett had made a point of befriending me. And bedding me.

"Why didn't Sandy tell me about you?"

The young man's cheeks flamed with color. "There are reasons—" He glanced at the door of Sandy's room. "I would not wish to tell you, if *he* felt it was not wise that I should do so."

"Sandy *told* you not to tell me?"

The boy nodded. "Yes, yes. There are reasons."

"Somebody tried to kill him last night! Your secret might have something—"

"If I could speak to him!" Dieter Strindberg placed a trembling hand on the wall.

"They're not going to let you talk to him! Not tonight! It's the cops you should—"

"No!" He backed away from me, shaking his head. "He would not wish it!"

Would not wish it. "This secret—is there a criminal penalty attached?"

The boy moistened his lips, swallowing.

"Sandy would want me to know!" I insisted. "Maybe he didn't before, but he would now!"

Dieter Strindberg just stood there.

"All right, listen. I've got to go home and get out of these clothes. Come with me. It's private there. Tell me only what you feel comfortable telling—"

"No, truly! I would prefer—I believe it is best—"

"To tell me nothing?"

"Please pardon me. No more than what I have already told you. Until I am sure . . ."

"That Sandy wants you to?"

"Yes, yes." He nodded emphatically.

I wondered whether the boy was afraid *for* Sandy, or *of* him.

A nurse wheeled a coughing old man down the corridor toward us, blitzing him with cheery small talk. He wheezed appreciatively, patting her hand.

I looked up at Dieter Strindberg. It wasn't like looking at Lennart. I was aware of the differences now. In me, too. "Come home with me anyway. We'll talk about the damn weather."

31

WE TOOK A cab to the Mayor's Residence, where I'd left my car some twenty hours earlier. I drove us over the squandered bricks of Old Town and across Highway 101, which dissected Hillsdale in the middle of its unintentionally art deco downtown. I noticed several news vans in front of the courthouse, and wondered if Captain Loftus had called a press conference. By the time we climbed a short hill to Clarke Street, Dieter Strindberg and I had already talked about the weather. It was raining again. Dieter said it reminded him of northern Germany, where he and Lennart had grown up. That was about all he said.

There weren't any news vans outside my house when I pulled up. I'd expected to see some. Sandy had been filmed leaving the house with me. Two hours later, he was lying on a stretcher. The press was bound to wonder why my friend—like my client and my neighbor before him—had been shot. The absence of a welcoming committee seemed to confirm my suspicion of a media event at the courthouse.

I left Dieter downstairs while I showered and changed out of my crumpled, muddied dress.

I had a great deal to think about, but mostly I thought about Hal. He hadn't come to the hospital to ask about Sandy. I'd expected a call, at least.

I remembered Captain Loftus saying Sandy should keep an eye on my cousin. I hoped the captain hadn't misinterpreted Hal's resentment of Sandy; I hoped he hadn't arrested Hal. I told myself I'd have heard from the family, if he had.

I was more afraid Hal had packed up and left town. His mother had sneered that he was allowed to camp in his hovel only because he was the mayor's son. Hal had spent years shedding his cloak of privilege; he wouldn't continue living there once he knew that.

If Hal had left town, I'd never find him. And it might be years before he drifted through San Francisco again. The thought made the blood throb in my temples, made my stomach feel like I'd swallowed a boulder.

I went back downstairs, wondering whether it was worth half an hour of slick road to confirm my fears.

Dieter Strindberg stood at the front window, holding open the old damask curtain. "There are large vehicles outside." He defined a box shape with his long hands. "With satellite dishes on the top."

"News vans. The police held some kind of press conference, I think. Now the reporters want my reaction." There was a loud rapping at my door. "You'd better stand away from the window."

He looked alarmed when I stepped into the hall. But I had no intention of answering the door.

I phoned my papa, and learned that no one in the family had seen Hal since he'd left the party.

"I'm trying to find my cousin," I explained to Dieter. "I'm going to drive out to where he's been living. You're welcome to come, if you want. Or I can drop you off wherever you're staying."

He eyed me suspiciously. Didn't want me to know where he was staying, I supposed.

I opened the door and spread my arms to keep Judy

Britt from entering. "I'm on my way out," I told her. She didn't budge.

A couple of reporters climbed out of their vans and dashed through the rain to my porch. One of them, a fat man with a clipped beard, said, "Do you think we could set up in your living room for five minutes? Get your reaction to the police captain's statement?"

I continued to bar the door. "What was the gist of his statement?"

The fat man pulled off a rain poncho, revealing a clip microphone with a logo I couldn't quite place. An Oregon station, I thought; southern Oregon, not too far away. The San Francisco stations would have recalled their troops by now; they had fires in Oakland to cover, child kidnappings in Fremont. They'd wait for an arrest before they came back. Until then, they'd rely on the likes of Judy Britt to keep them abreast.

"Can we come in?" repeated the man.

"What did Loftus say?"

Behind him, an older man sneezed. I recognized him. Anchorman of the local news for the last thirty years.

Judy Britt spoke. She looked like an Eskimo in her fake-fur fringed hood. "He identified Sander Arkelett as a San Francisco detective who was apparently working for you. He said Arkelett was shot twice from about twenty feet with a thirty-eight caliber gun. He wouldn't say whether he had any suspects." It was clear from her tone whom *she* suspected.

"Let us in," the fat man coaxed. "We have to say *something*—and you don't want us speculating. A brief statement, that's all."

Dieter stood in the living room doorway, just out of the reporters' sight. I grabbed his hand, and pulled him outside, firmly slamming the door behind us.

I tried to tug him down the porch stairs before anyone could block our path, but Dieter let go of my hand. He stood chin to forehead with the fat reporter, looking aghast, like a deer caught in the glare of headlights. I had to go back and push him from behind, bulldozing the reporter aside. In the meantime, a huge light was trained on us from inside the Oregon news vans.

We were both soaked by the time I shoved Dieter into the Mercedes. A man sat cross-legged inside the news van, filming the scene. He would probably report that I'd fled guiltily.

As I went around to the driver's side, I noticed Gary Gleason standing at his front window looking out at me, gesturing and shaking his head.

I looked at my ex-husband, then looked behind me at the reporters. I didn't know what Gary was driving at, and I didn't feel like crossing the street in the rain to find out.

I broke a few speed limits racing toward the jetty.

I tried to get Dieter to talk—talk about anything—as a prelude to asking him a few questions. But the boy was determinedly monosyllabic. I shot through the cannery district, past the Victorians of Hillsdale's founding despoilers. I slowed down as we negotiated the long, slick curve of road beside the murky bay. My wipers weren't fast enough to keep the windshield clear.

It took about twenty minutes to reach what had once been hundreds of acres of waterfowl refuge, and was now a sinking housing development.

As I'd feared, Hal's house was dark. My headlights reflected off the waterlogged plywood that covered the windows, and I noticed that two or three boards had been nailed across the front door. One of them bore an ancient, weatherbeaten condemnation notice.

"Damn! Damn it!" I cried, pounding the car horn in frustration. Its cheerful peeping was barely audible; the convertible top magnified the pounding of the rain like a drumskin.

I reached into the small baggage space behind the bucket

seats, groping for my flashlight. I wasn't willing to admit to myself that Hal was really gone. I had a vague thought of breaking into the house to see if he'd left anything behind to show he meant to come back.

I grabbed a cold metal object and pulled it out of the compartment. I didn't notice it wasn't a flashlight until Dieter Strindberg drew in his breath and fumbled for the door handle. Then I looked at the object in my hand and saw it was the goddamned disappearing gun.

I let out a stream of expletives that would have shocked a longshoreman; they certainly set my passenger to trembling.

I immediately regretted my display of temper. Dieter was already skittish, already leery of me. And here I was flashing a gun and screeching like a fishwife.

I was about to put the gun down and explain, when Dieter cried, ''You have known who I am! You have lied!''

''Who you are? You're—'' I realized he was telling me that he *wasn't*.

The dashboard lights glinted green on his colorless hair and pale skin, making him look almost otherworldly.

And it occurred to me that I was out in the middle of nowhere with a man I knew nothing about, except that he closely resembled someone I'd once known.

I held the gun in both hands, carefully, as if it were a smoldering powder keg. I'd never checked to see if it was loaded; I didn't know how. I made sure my fingers didn't touch the trigger. ''You're not Lennart's brother,'' I said, trying to sound as if I knew who he was, as well as who he wasn't.

The boy bent his head, staring at the gun. He murmured something. I strained to hear him over the drumbeat of rain.

''Lennart had no brother. We invented one, Sander Arkelett and myself.''

I was about to protest that I'd seen Lennart's will, but I

realized that it hadn't mentioned anyone but Kirsten. It was Sandy who told me the will had disinherited a brother.

The boy's voice became plaintive. "You will not take me to the police?"

"Why did Sandy lie to me? Why did he want me to think Lennart had a brother?"

The gun seemed to weigh ten pounds. It was cold and slippery and repulsive to the touch. I thought of Wallace Bean; he'd loved his forty-five. He'd confided in a pretrial interview that he found "his piece" sexy—and that he felt sexy firing it.

My passenger seemed to misinterpret my fidgeting preoccupation with the revolver. He was out of the car before I could attempt to stop him (though I wasn't sure I wanted to stop him). He disappeared behind a curtain of rain, sprinting toward the jetty.

I slammed the passenger door shut, mechanically wiping rainwater from the leather seat. The boy looked so damned much like Lennart; who the hell could he be? Lennart would have been thirty-three if he'd lived; too young to have so old a son.

Perhaps the boy was an actor, hired because of his resemblance to Lennart Strindberg. And yet, the resemblance was more than superficial; it was in his voice, in his gait.

I looked for the boy as I drove out to the main road, but I saw no sign of him. The storm was particularly ferocious on that outcropping of rock and sand, miles from town. But I supposed "Dieter" had enough sense to take shelter in one of the decaying monuments to my Uncle Henry's bad judgment.

Sooner or later, the storm would abate and he would walk back to town. I wondered what, if anything, I should do about it.

32

As I DROVE toward Hillsdale, I puzzled over the boy's panicky flight into the rain. True, I'd pulled a gun out of the baggage well and done some serious swearing, but the boy's reaction seemed unduly paranoid. He'd assumed I'd pulled a gun on him because I knew who he was. And he'd run out into a rainstorm, fearing my reaction.

But he couldn't have been afraid of *me*, or he wouldn't have risked a bullet in the back by diving out of the car that way.

He'd been afraid I'd turn him over to the police. He'd said as much.

I didn't think the boy had shot Sandy—at the hospital, he'd seemed genuinely distraught. And, assuming his accent was authentic, I didn't see what possible connection a young German could have to Wallace Bean.

So who were the police seeking in connection with Kirsten's murder?

I'd handled enough murder trials to know that the police always look for the person who stands to benefit financially from a murder.

But surely Gary Gleason would inherit Kirsten's property. That building of hers in San Francisco's financial district was not community property (inheritances are always separate property), but Kirsten must have bequeathed it to Gary. People with valuable assets usually make wills—if they're married to beneficiary lawyers.

I remembered Captain Loftus asking me about Kirsten's "papers"; I'd assumed—feared—he referred to Kirsten's letters. But maybe he'd been trying to track down a missing will. Gary would have told the police that Kirsten had made one, and the captain would have become suspicious if a police search failed to locate it. Maybe that's why the warrant to search my house had authorized the police to look for anything written by or to or about Kirsten Strindberg. Maybe the cops had wondered whether I hated my ex-husband enough to do him out of his inheritance.

The thought fascinated me, stayed with me for miles of dark, wet road.

What if the boy I'd known as Dieter Strindberg were Kirsten's heir under the laws of intestate succession? What if he were *Kirsten's*, and not Lennart's, next of kin?

I let a stoplight go green, then red, then green again, thinking about it.

I'd assumed Kirsten and Lennart had been married because they'd had the same last name. But Kirsten hadn't taken Gary's name when she'd married *him*.

Maybe Kirsten hadn't taken Lennart's name either, maybe she hadn't had to. Maybe the two of them had been cousins, like me and Hal. That would explain why Dieter Strindberg (if that was his name) resembled Lennart.

And the boy might have been entitled to some share of the estate, had Lennart died intestate. That would explain why the boy had hired Sandy. Kirsten's financial district property had become a hundred times more valuable since the old leases had expired—ample incentive for the boy to check the circumstances of Lennart's death.

A car horn behind me urged me to do less thinking and more driving. I sped through the intersection and pulled off the road. The rain had slackened to a drizzle, shrouding the decommissioned power plant across the bay in twinkling mist. Thousands of tiny lights reflected on a mirror of black mud, creating the illusion of a romantic—if potentially lethal—fairy castle.

My bit of guesswork seemed all right as far as it went. It explained why the boy had panicked, thinking I'd discovered his identity. I might have taken him to the police at gunpoint, telling them he was Kirsten's next of kin. If the young German had been in town the night of Kirsten's murder, Loftus would probably have arrested him first and asked questions later.

But my theory didn't explain why Sandy had lied to me about the boy being Lennart's younger brother. Sandy could have told me the truth; the boy's relationship to Kirsten would have made little difference to my plan.

I could only suppose that telling me the truth would have altered Sandy's plan.

I felt my forehead, hoping to find signs of feverishness. I wanted to believe that my suspicions were irrational; that Sander Arkelett had *not* been hired by Kirsten Strindberg's next of kin to steal her will and murder her.

33

I DIDN'T THINK there was much likelihood Hal had shown up at his parents' house, but I drove there anyway.

By the time I pulled up to the mock chalet, the rain had stopped, though the wind continued to rock my convertible. I locked the passenger door and climbed out. A dripping plastic police cordon stretched around my aunt's rhododendron bushes, but I didn't see any cops. I supposed they were waiting for daylight to complete their search—they'd wait forever if they were waiting for good weather.

I was getting ready to ring the doorbell when my Uncle Henry opened the door. He was startled to see me, nearly dropping the overnight bag he carried.

Recovering, he took my elbow and steered me down the porch steps. "You have your car, don't you, Laura? Give me a lift."

"Is Hal here?"

My uncle shook his head, glancing nervously at the upstairs windows.

I unlocked the passenger door for him, automatically tossing his small bag into the baggage well—right on top of the revolver. I silently cursed my stupidity. I'd have to remember to get the bag out before my uncle did. "Has Hal been here today? Or anytime since the party?"

"Huh! If you could hear what she says to him! No, no, he never comes here."

I climbed in and started the car. "Where to?"

He was still looking back at the house, fiddling distractedly with the buttons of his jacket.

"Uncle Henry?"

"Oh, I don't know. A hotel?"

In the dim light of a street lamp, he looked a great deal like my papa. The resemblance was particularly pronounced because my uncle wasn't affecting his usual jovial, political twinkle.

I remembered my aunt telling Sandy at the party that my uncle was ill. And he did look different; not ill, perhaps, but distressed.

I eased out of my parking place. "You can stay at my house. I've got five spare bedrooms—two of them even have beds."

My uncle merely nodded. He looked so lost in his own troubles that I nearly spared him mine. Thank God I didn't.

I hesitated, then pressed him, "Do you have any idea where Hal could be?"

My uncle shook his head glumly. "She calls him an idiot, a mental deficient—her own son. To his face. No, he doesn't visit us, not for years at a time."

"Do you think he's gone off again?"

"My son lives like a hobo, but she won't help him because she's ashamed. She wants promises he won't give her."

"What's the matter with Hal, Uncle Henry? Something happened to him in the war, didn't it?"

"She didn't even tell *me*. My only boy. He could have died and me not even knowing he'd been shot." His voice was thick, probably inebriated. "I find out years later from a damned army doctor who's passing through town!"

"Find out *what*? When was Hal shot? Where?"

"In the head. Left hemisphere damage, the doctor says. Very serious, he says. And for thirteen years, she's keeping it a secret. Because it wasn't in the line of duty."

"What does that mean?"

"I don't know. She won't say and Henry won't, either." He raised his hand in a gesture of despair. "But what *could* it mean, Laura? Suicide attempt, that's all it could mean."

We rode the rest of the way in silence. Left hemisphere damage. I'd had a physiology course at San Francisco State, a decade ago. I still remembered some of the basics. Enough to make sense of a few things I'd noticed. Enough to scare the hell out of me.

Judy Britt and the sixty-year-old anchorman were no longer on my porch when I pulled up in front of my house. The Oregon van still lingered, though, its doors shut tight and its windows steamed over. I guessed they needed an interview to justify their junket. The fat reporter rolled

down the passenger window as I walked past, but I forestalled his question with a grumpy, "Forget it!"

My uncle and I went inside. He went off to find my
liquor, and I unfolded a square of paper that had been
slipped through the mail slot of my old-fashioned front
door.

My uncle found me still standing in the hallway puz-
zling over it.

"Want a snort yourself?" he asked, holding up a liter
of Johnny Walker.

"Look at this." I handed him the note, which appeared
to have been scrawled quickly, in printed capitals.

The note read: *Laura, I need to talk to you about Sandy.
Meet me in his room. It's after visiting hours, but you can
get in through his window if you climb the fire escape. It's
important. Come as soon as you can. Hal.*

My uncle frowned as he read the note. "I don't know,
Laura. Do you think you should?"

"No, I definitely shouldn't." I stuffed the note into my
trouser pocket. "Where the hell did I put my coat?"

34

I LOCATED MY herringbone wool coat. It was the only
article of clothing I had with pockets big enough to hold
a gun.

I climbed into the Mercedes and checked the baggage

well behind my seat. For once, the goddamned revolver was exactly where I'd left it. I didn't dare turn on the interior light to examine it, not with a van full of reporters a few hundred feet away; but I held it in my palm, forced myself to wrap my finger around the trigger. I remembered Hal saying to me, when Kirsten had the gun, that I should be careful because it was cocked. I found what I supposed was the cock, a trigger-shaped affair above the handgrip. If worse came to worst, I would make a show of cocking the gun and aiming it. I knew I'd never be able to shoot.

I remembered the film footage of Senators Hansen and Dzhura being knocked backward, then crumpling forward on those airplane steps. How many times had I down-played the effect of Bean's act? How many times had I begged the jury to focus on poor, sick Wally Bean and forget about Harley Hansen and Garth Dzhura?

I tried to fit the gun into my coat pocket, but the barrel was too long. I ended up tearing a hole in the pocket and sliding the barrel into the coat's lining. The damned thing was so heavy; I hoped it wouldn't rip through.

I engaged the engine and turned on the lights, then looked across the street. Once again, my ex-husband stood at the front window, watching me through parted curtains. His silhouette was distorted by water rippling down the glass.

Gary Gleason had been watching my house. He'd seen me leave with Kirsten's next of kin. And he knew I had come to town to exact revenge on him and his wife; I'd told him so myself. Did he think I'd conspired with the boy to murder Kirsten? To steal her will?

The note—Gary had seen it pushed through my mail slot. He'd also seen me come home, stay inside long enough to read it, and then go back out to my car.

I noticed that Gary's Peugeot was no longer in its car-port. It was parked on the street in front of the house. Gary Gleason was planning to follow me, I was certain.

I turned off the headlights, cut the engine, and walked across the street.

Gary opened the door before I knocked.

He wore a plain brown sweater, jeans, and running shoes. He was pale and his posture was stiff. He was frowning, but it wasn't his usual busy man's frown; he looked like he was in pain. He was clean-shaven (except for his rust-colored mustache), but his frizzy brown hair looked slightly damp or slightly dirty.

"I saw you coming," he said to me.

I nodded. "Did you hear about Sandy Arkelett?"

"Yeah. They said on the news he was a private detective, working for you."

"I thought he was working for me. But he might have been working for that boy you saw me with earlier."

A vein in Gary's forehead stood out in blue, throbbing relief. "Do you know who he is?"

"Kirsten's relative."

"What's he doing here?" Gary's tone seethed with suspicion. "Do the police know he's here?"

"They do now, I'm sure," I said dryly.

Gary took a step backward. "Yeah, I called the cops. She was my *wife*, what do you expect?"

"I don't care who you called. I met him for the first time this evening at the hospital." I pulled the recently delivered note out of my pocket. "Here. Look at this."

My ex-husband's breathing grew labored, reading it. He could draw his own conclusions—just as long as he didn't guess mine.

He handed it back. "So?"

I could see the Peugeot out of the corner of my eye. "So there's been too much shooting around here lately." It was more difficult—and more galling—than I'd thought it would be, asking this of Gary. "I don't want to go there by myself."

Gary regarded me warily. "You want *me* to go with you?"

Better than having you follow me, you bastard. "Maybe you're not up to it."

I saw the conflicting emotions in my ex-husband's eyes. But I knew he'd say yes. He'd always courted the appearance of nobility—when it didn't prejudice his likelihood of getting what he wanted.

"No, I'm all right. I'll get my jacket."

I stepped inside while he went upstairs. I could feel the revolver strain the lining of my coat. I slipped my hand into my pocket and held the gun, relieving the tension on the seam. I told myself I was making a dangerous situation safer, that it really was better this way. But part of me was too angry to care about safety; I felt my finger slide over the trigger. Startled, I let the gun drop back into the lining.

There were stacks of books all over the floor of Gary's living room; the ceiling-high bookcase was nearly empty. The drawers of a built-in hutch had been emptied, and papers were sorted into untidy piles. Gary had kept Kirsten's will at his office, I supposed, with a second copy at home. If the original had vanished from its file, he'd be searching the house for the copy.

When Gary joined me, I said, with as much sympathy as I could feign, "Captain Loftus told me your office was burglarized."

"*Loftus* told you?" He spoke the name sneeringly.

"Yes."

Gary slipped awkwardly into his jacket, glancing at me. "You sure you heard it from Loftus?"

"It might have been one of the other cops," I lied again, opening the front door for him.

As he walked past me, I experienced a jolt of *déjà vu*: holding the door of an apartment Gary and I had joyfully decorated with upside-down American flags. It hit me like a rabbit punch that we'd been happy there.

I slammed Gary's front door behind us.

To my relief, the Oregon reporter remained in his van while we crossed the street to my car. I didn't want to be filmed with my son-of-a-bitch ex-husband.

Gary stared silently out the passenger window all the way to County Hospital.

I parked in the front parking lot, and walked up to the double glass front doors. Gary hung back, watching indecisively, before following me.

We checked in with a wizened woman at the front desk. She told us firmly that visiting hours were over.

I said, "We're not here to visit. We're here to see one of the nurses upstairs." I turned to my frowning companion. "What's her name again, Gary?"

With only a slight hesitation, Gary supplied the name of a nurse he'd presumably met during his sojourn at the hospital.

The woman told us to sign in and go on up, then. I signed both our names on a numbered and lined sheet of paper. I scanned the sheet. Hal's name wasn't on it. But then, I hadn't expected it to be.

We rode the elevator upstairs, and Gary remarked on my resourcefulness in getting past the desk. It seemed to displease him.

At the nurses' station, I announced, "My name is Laura Di Palma. Sander Arkelett was working for me when he got shot, and I have reason to believe someone's still after him. Right now. Tonight."

The two nurses looked up from their disordered stacks of paperwork. They looked harried, tired, and unwilling to listen to anything that might mean more work for them. A light on a board began to blink, and one of them complained, "Oh, cripes! Not Mrs. P. again!"

The other nurse, a young girl with a sallow, acned complexion, said to her companion, "It's your turn." She watched the older woman roll her eyes and trot off down the hall. Then she turned back to me. "Well, what do you expect *us* to do?"

"I want you to check Mr. Arkelett's room right now and make sure no one's in there. Then I want you to check the window that opens onto the fire escape and make sure it's locked."

The girl looked skeptical. "No one's up here but us!"

"Check."

"I can't leave till Nina gets back."

It seemed pointless to argue. I led Gary to the bench upon which I'd spent the previous night.

He said, "I thought you got along pretty well with your cousin Hal."

I nodded, avoiding his eye.

"But you don't trust him?"

I didn't respond.

Gary stroked his mustache thoughtfully. "He always was hard to figure. There's been a lot of talk about him around town, since he's the mayor's son." His hand dropped from his mustache, his jaw clamped; he bore the mayor no good will. "People say he got shell-shocked or something; that he's been a little strange since the war."

"A head wound," I confirmed.

The other nurse returned from Mrs. P.'s room. I stood up, and the acned girl, with a whispered explanation that left her co-worker snickering, said, "Okay, let's take a look."

Sandy lay in semidarkness, hooked up to his monitors and plastic bottles, his eyes closed. He made a rasping sound in his throat.

I stood beside the bed, frightened and revolted by the tubes taped to his face. The nurse made a big show of looking around the room. A smile hovered on her lips; she and her helpmate would have a good laugh, later.

Then she walked to the window across from Sandy's bed, and pushed up on the sash. The window opened.

The nurse had her back to me, but I heard her mutter, "Gosh darn!" as she closed and locked it.

I walked to the door, where Gary stood watching. He said, "What do you suppose your cousin wanted?"

"I don't know."

"Are you going to ask him?"

"If I can find him."

His expression noble, my ex-husband said, "You'd better let me come with you."

35

"Where does your cousin live?"

I fumbled for my car keys. Part of my object had been achieved: Sandy's room was secure.

"He's been camping out in a house near the jetty." I was conscious of the weight of the gun in my coat. If I timed things right—"In that abandoned housing development."

Gary whistled. "Sounds like he's got problems. What exactly—"

I cut him off. "I want to check my uncle's house before I drive all the way out there."

Out of the corner of my eye, I saw Gary touch his sweater gingerly, as if checking his ribs. I remembered a nurse telling me he could have gone home the morning after his accident. Maybe even the same night? Through the unlocked hospital window, and down the fire escape?

When we pulled up in front of the Mayor's Residence, I told him I'd leave the heater on for him. Then I slammed the door behind me, the motor still running.

My papa answered the door, wearing the smoking jacket I'd given him the Christmas before. He smoothed his hair crankily, his face twitching with irritation.

"Thank goodness!" He pulled me inside. "Come and say *something* to your aunt. She's . . ." He waved his arm; there didn't seem to be words for what my aunt was.

I found Aunt Diana pacing her gilded living room, fists clenched, shedding furious tears. At the sight of me, she erupted into a brief diatribe, the gist of which was that my uncle would find out he couldn't throw her away like an old shoe, not after she'd made him everything that he was. "Everyone knows I'm *ten* times better qualified to be mayor than he is!"

"Run against him," I suggested. "You've got the contacts."

My aunt looked at me as though I were some biblical abomination. "*I* don't have to act like a man to prove *my* worth!"

I glanced at my papa. His expression said, *You see what I've had to put up with.*

"Well, I'm staying right here," my aunt raged. "If he thinks he can shame me into moving . . ." She resumed pacing.

"I'm sure the town bylaws don't *require* the mayor to live here, but you should find out if they stipulate an alternate use for the house if he chooses not to."

My aunt swallowed several times before she was able to say, "If I need advice, I'll find a lawyer with a better reputation than yours, missy!"

Pity I couldn't find an aunt with a better disposition than hers.

I took my papa's arm and steered him out of the room. I told him Uncle Henry was at my house.

"After forty years of marriage!" My papa shook his head. "Henry must be crazy!"

"Papa, did Aunt Diana ever tell you what happened to Hal in the war?"

My papa was frowning at the living room door. His tone was distracted. "I wish you'd call him Henry. What kind of a name is Hal?" Then he looked at me. "I've heard them fighting about him lately."

"I think Aunt Diana has known for a long time what's the matter with Hal; I think the army must have notified her when it happened. But she didn't want anyone to know about it because she thought it was too—" I had to stop and take a breath; she was such an infuriating woman. "I don't know, embarrassing. From what I gather, Uncle Henry just ran into an army doctor who treated Hal for a head wound—"

"A head wound!" My papa looked skeptical. "I never heard anything about a head wound!"

"That's the point!"

My papa paled, his swarthy skin lightening to yellow. "No, no. A mother doesn't keep a secret like that from the family."

"I saw Hal's Purple Heart myself. And Uncle Henry claims the doctor says Hal had—" I hated to say it; it hurt even to think about it. "That he has brain damage."

"But he seems—!" Papa stopped; Hal did *not* seem normal. "What kind of damage?"

"Hal won't talk about it. Apparently Aunt Diana won't either."

"Brain damage." My papa looked back at the living room door, his brows knit. "The boy should have told us himself! We would have—"

"I know. We would have." I felt a great weariness of spirit. "Hal didn't want us to. He doesn't like us well enough."

I left my papa shaking his head, as if mere denial could pull our family together.

I went upstairs to make two phone calls.

36

GARY HAD TURNED off the car motor. He sat shivering with cold in the passenger seat.

"You should have left the heater on," I observed. "I have plenty of gas."

Gary mumbled something about not knowing how long I was going to be inside.

I made a point of catching his eye, which seemed to take him aback. I started the engine, but switched off the heater.

Then I pulled out of my parking space and cruised slowly past my papa's Lincoln.

"I shouldn't have done it," I admitted, "but when Kirsten went with you in the ambulance, I snooped around your house a little bit."

Gary muttered, "Christ!"

"Your back porch was really a mess."

Gary made no response, but he breathed like an angry man.

I drove us out to the jetty. I drove past the ghostly housing development that had displaced all the egrets, and lately housed my antisocial cousin. I crossed the expanse of hard-packed sand separating the houses from the rocky tip of the jetty, and I parked the car. We were a few hundred feet from the huge, jagged rocks that snaked out to sea.

There might have been a moon; it was too overcast to tell. The rocks were visible only as a darker shade of black against the gray-black sky. The sea, wild from the week's storms, battered the rocks, sending up a cloud of salt spray that coated my windshield, sheeting off in thin rivulets.

Gary's voice was gruff. "I thought you said your cousin was camping in one of those houses back there."

"No lights. So if he's here at all, he's sitting out on the rocks."

I heard Gary fumble for the door handle, and I reached across and stopped him, pulling his wrist back. "No. If Hal's here, I want to talk to him alone. I'll make him come out where you can see us from the car, but I want to talk to him alone."

I switched the motor back on, and turned on the headlights. Mist swirled in the double tunnel of light.

The dashboard lights lit Gary's face from the bottom up, illuminating a pronounced frown.

I reached forward and turned on the heater. Then I climbed quickly out of the car, slamming the door behind me.

37

ALMOST AS SOON as I walked past the misty glow of my headlights, I stumbled into Hal.

At first, I was ecstatic. I slipped my arms around his neck and kissed him. His response was gratifying.

Then I remembered my errand. I backed away. The wind whistled over the flats, stinging my face with needles of sand and flecks of sea foam.

"What are you doing here, Hal?" He was just a dark shape, even at arm's length. I reached into my coat for the gun, pulling it up and sideways, until most of it was in my pocket, barrel dangling into the coat lining. "Your house is all boarded up."

"I didn't hear about Sandy till a few hours ago," he said over the wail of wind and pounding of waves. "I went by your house—you weren't there. I tried the hospital— dragon lady downstairs didn't want to let me in. I went up anyway, but you weren't there. So I phoned your place—" Even shouting, he sounded puzzled. "My dad said you were coming out here. To the jetty."

"How'd you get here so fast?"

"Caught a ride to the turnoff. What are you doing way the hell out here?"

"Did Uncle Henry tell you about the note? That I went to the hospital to meet you?"

I listened to the sea hammer the rocks, listened to the wind shriek between them. It seemed a long time before Hal answered. "He said you got a note from me. But, Laura—"

"I knew it wasn't from you." I glanced behind me, at the arcs of light from my headlamps. "Gary's with me."

"Gleason? Why?"

"I told him I was looking for you. I'm going to say I didn't find you."

"What the hell would I be doing out here? And what did you bring Gleason for? You're not *afraid* of me?"

"Look Hal, if we're going to talk, let's get behind—" I started toward the rocks, but my cousin grabbed my arm. Even through two layers of wool, his grip was painful.

"My dad said you asked him to—"

At that moment, Gary Gleason manuevered my car so that the headlights swept across the sand and caught us standing there, me trying to pull free of Hal's grasp.

I looked at Hal, turning my back on the Mercedes.

His face was starkly white in the glare of the headlights. "Why did you bring Gleason? Why *him*, of all—?"

"He'll be here in a second! Damn it, Hal—use your head!"

"What's left of it?"

I should have remembered my plan; acted in accordance with it. But the pain in Hal's voice paralyzed me. I reached out, in the spotlight of my own headlights, and caressed my cousin's cheek.

And then it was too late. Gary Gleason stood in the circle of light with us, his frizzy hair glowing like a halo.

He looked from Hal to me. His face was taut with anger. "You're not afraid of him!" he said, barely loud enough for me to hear. "That's not why you brought me here, is it? All this crap with your heater; what the hell are you up to? Bringing me all the way out here!"

"I was looking for Hal," I insisted. I glanced at my

cousin, warning him not to deny it. But Hal was staring at a point near Gary's belt buckle. He reached toward it, then froze. Slowly, still staring, he lowered the extended arm.

Gary was saying, "What are you trying to prove, Laura? That you know how we did it?"

I followed Hal's gaze. My ex-husband held a small, short-barreled black gun.

I slipped my hand into my pocket. *Please, God, let me have timed things right.* "Did what?"

"Never mind. Forget it. Why'd you drag me out to the hospital?"

I stared at my ex-husband's gun. In my mind's eye, I saw them again, Senators Hansen and Dzhura, walking down the airplane steps, waving. Looking startled. Falling.

Two men dead, and I hadn't allowed myself—or the jury—to care.

"I wanted you to know it wasn't safe," I told Gary. "Whatever you were planning. I wanted you to know that Sandy's window was locked and that the nurses were alerted."

"How did you know the note was from me?" The wind and waves were louder than Gary's voice, but I heard him— almost to the exclusion of other sounds. The gun was a powerful hearing aid.

"You'd stayed in the same hospital room as Sandy; you knew the window was unlocked. Also, your view of my house. You knew when I was gone, when you could leave me a note."

My ex-husband ran a hand over his wind-whipped halo of hair. "Come on, Laura! Your cousin could have gone to the hospital and fooled with the window, for all you knew. And I saw him knock on your door tonight; that's why I signed his name. How'd you know *he* didn't leave the note?"

Gary's gun was steady. I stared at the barrel like a mouse at a snake. Sick or not, what the hell right did Bean have—

My cousin answered for me. "I can't read or write."

"Hal!" I'd been right; but it still felt like he'd slapped me.

"Bullshit!" Gary's voice rang with exasperation. "Of course you can—"

"I caught a bullet in the head in Vietnam." My cousin's voice was lower in pitch than I'd ever heard it. "Four-year-olds read better than me."

The wind seemed to screech with malevolence. The reading and writing center of the brain is in the left hemisphere; I'd remembered that. And I'd remembered the dearth of books and magazines in Hal's house.

And other things. My cousin's income tax forms: hard to apply for jobs if you can't write, impossible to get any but the most menial if you can't read. No driver's license; not without taking a renewal exam. Even the Thorazine: a way to cope with long nights without books, magazines, or newspapers; with being unable to send or receive letters; with being unable to read price tags or bus schedules or street signs. Undrugged—as Hal claimed to be—it would be easy to fall into the habit of brooding, to drink too much and grow bitter.

Such an evil weapon, the gun.

I looked at Gary's gun, wondering if it was a thirty-eight. Wondering if it had blown holes in Sandy's chest. "What would you have done at the hospital, if you'd had me and Sandy alone?"

"Put this gun to your detective's head, and asked you then what I'm going to ask you now."

I couldn't see my ex-husband very well. Hal and I faced the headlights; Gary's back was to them. I could only hope his attention was directed to my face. I wrapped my fingers around the grip of the Buntline Scout. The gun was warmer than my numb hand, awkward to hold. I knew what Gary was going to ask me, and I knew he wouldn't like my answer.

"You fell off your roof while you were cleaning your rain gutter," I said, just to say something. I inched the Scout out of my coat pocket. "My papa didn't run over you. You just said that to warn me off."

I felt exposed and vulnerable in the glare of the lights, with a huge revolver dangling from my hand. I didn't know how to cock the gun and shoot it—I wasn't sure I would, even if I could. And Gary was smart. Smart enough to observe my fumbling revulsion and realize I didn't know how to shoot. But if I could keep him focused on my face and my words, I might be able to pass the gun to Hal. In Hal's hands, the gun would be a potent threat.

I continued hastily, "I was sure you were lying about my papa when you didn't repeat your accusation to anyone else; lawyers tend to be careful about slander. Then the other day I saw someone cleaning out a rain gutter with a stick, and I remembered what I'd seen in your back yard. There was a broken plant on the step, and above it, under your rain gutter, there was a macramé plant hanger with a two-by-two stuck in the mesh. It occurred to me that maybe you'd climbed your porch railing and pulled yourself onto the roof to clean your rain gutter with the two-by-two—you're a local, you probably knew a storm was coming. I remembered that Kirsten's needlepoint was on the floor near the back door, like she'd gone running out there in a hurry. It wasn't near the front door, like it should have been if she'd run out front because of an accident."

I held the gun behind me, out of Gary's line of sight. I wiggled it a bit, trying to catch Hal's eye.

Gary's tone was sardonic. "So I fall off the roof, then I hobble around to the front of my house, for some nefarious reason of my own."

"I'd made you nervous at my office-warming party, talking about Lennart, telling you I had my own detective, that I knew about Kirsten's property in San Francisco, that I'd moved into a house across the street from yours. You wanted me to think you had something on me, too; you wanted me to think you could blackmail me, if you chose to. You weren't hurt badly—a nurse at the hospital told me so. And yet Kirsten called everyone she could think of—ambulance, cops, fire department. You knew I was due home any minute to meet you at my house, and you were putting on a show for me. You wanted to implicate my father—but only to me. You wanted to scare me. To keep me quiet about Lennart.''

Gary said, "You'll never prove it wasn't a hit-and-run.''

He was right about that, and we both knew it. But then, I hadn't wanted to make Gary feel threatened. Not while he was pointing a gun at my belly. I'd been playing for time, trying to avoid the inevitable question.

But it came, anyway. "Where the hell is my wife's will?''

It was now or never. I had to find a way to make Hal notice the gun. Gary would never believe I hadn't purloined that will. I believed he'd murdered Lennart; of course I'd want to deprive him of Lennart's money.

I said, apropos of nothing, "Tonight my Aunt Diana said I was slumming it with the local boys.''

I saw my ex-husband shake his head, perplexed. I didn't dare glance at Hal, didn't dare do anything that might make Gary Gleason look away from my face.

But I knew the statement would make Hal look at me—not at Gary, not at Gary's gun. At me. I raised the gun several inches behind my back, extending it toward Hal.

I said, "The will wasn't with Kirsten's letters, Gary. If you haven't found it, she must have destroyed it herself. Maybe she felt guilty.''

I didn't believe that. Gary wouldn't either.

I'm sorry, senators, I prayed. *I was only doing my job.*

I was startled when Hal's fingers brushed mine. I jerked

involuntarily, and Gary's gun came up suddenly. Behind my back, the other gun, my gun, was wrested from my hand; and something—Hal's fist—slammed into my shoulder, pitching me sideways onto the sand. I landed painfully, blinded by grit. A twist of driftwood sliced my cheek.

There was a blast. It sounded like a bomb, but I knew it was a gunshot. I heard it echo in the rocks. I smelled burnt powder.

I tried to blink the sand and smoke out of my eyes, tried to use the Mercedes headlights as a landmark. I had to see whether my cousin was still standing.

As I scrambled to my knees, one of the men—I was too disoriented to know which—leapt over me. A second later, both of them hit the wet beach, covering me in a blizzard of damp sand. I could heard their grunting battle, but I wasn't sure which was topmost.

Before I could orient myself, one of them was back on his feet.

38

"IT'S OKAY," HAL panted. "It's okay, Laura. I've got both guns."

I squinted up at him, my eyes stinging with sand. Beside me, Gary Gleason lay on his back, knees tucked up, hugging his ribs and coughing.

"Point one at him, Hal," I shouted over the roar of wind against rock. "He killed Lennart Strindberg, and by God he's going to admit it."

I knelt beside my ex-husband. My knees sank a few inches into the icy sand. The surface layer swirled around me, pelting my cheeks, whistling past my ears. "You were stupid to stage that hit-and-run, Gary. Once I realized you'd done that, I was sure you'd killed Lennart. You wouldn't have been so determined to shut me up, otherwise."

My ex-husband lay still, clutching his side.

"It was mean-spirited of you to involve poor John Loftus! To rig an exhaust leak you knew they'd blame on your mechanic!" I remembered Captain Loftus quietly praising his son for dying in Vietnam; praiseworthy or not, the sacrifice had been unnecessary. "John had been in trouble before for screwing up an exhaust system, and he'd just worked on the VW. He was a convenient scapegoat—and you'd never forgiven him for shooting out the Peace Center's windows with his BB gun."

Gary sat up, looking behind me. Our positions were reversed now; he faced the headlights. His fierce wariness satisfied me that Hal was indeed pointing a gun at him.

I continued, "You booby-trapped the VW's exhaust system; you rigged it so carbon monoxide flowed in through the heater. Then you had Kirsten pick up Lennart in our car. She probably told him she was going to reconcile with him, but that she needed to tell you first. Then she drove him to wherever you were staying, and left him in the car with the heater running while she went inside, supposedly to talk to you. You two must have sat in there—how long? five, ten minutes?—waiting for Lennart to be overcome by the fumes."

Gary didn't look at me; he continued looking over my shoulder. I glanced back and saw the glint of gunmetal.

"You always were the practical one, Gary. Idealistic,

too, in a hip sort of way, but practical enough to keep your affair with Kirsten a secret until Lennart had made a will in her favor. While you lived with me, my father helped you financially. When you moved in with Kirsten, you needed a new sugar daddy. And Lennart was it. His money spared you the drudgery of a menial job like John Loftus's. It gave you the wherewithal to educate yourself, so you could be a committed young lawyer, staging sit-ins to save the egrets.''

Gary transferred his gaze to my face. But he said nothing, admitted nothing.

''You must have been furious when Lennart left the car to go find a phone booth and call me at the motel.''

I watched him scowl, start to speak, hesitate. He clutched at straws, like any trial lawyer faced with damning evidence. ''You say you got a phone call at the motel at midnight. The police report says Lennart was dead at eleven forty-five.''

''Captain Loftus must have altered the police report. When he found Lennart dead in the VW, out here near the jetty,'' I looked at its black, craggy outline against the lighter sky, ''when he realized Lennart had been asphyxiated by exhaust, he must have panicked. His son repaired Volkswagens, and he'd screwed up an exhaust system before. I think the captain drove into town, got a hose, came back and ran it from the exhaust pipe into the car. I think he changed the police records to read that he'd found the body at eleven forty-five, in case anyone had seen him in town after midnight, picking up the hose and the hardware he needed.''

''I thought, according to your scenario, that the Volkswagen was parked in front of my place.'' My ex-husband's tone managed to be both supercilious and conciliatory.

''It was, but when Lennart turned off the engine and went to call me, you and Kirsten had to think of an alternate plan. When Lennart got back, he found you waiting for him in the Volkswagen. You probably said you wanted to talk to him—he was too nice a person to say no. So you drove him out to the jetty, then made an excuse to leave the car, just like I did a while ago. You turned on the heater and walked away. You waited until Lennart passed out, then you shifted him into the driver's seat. You locked the car with the engine running and the heater still on. Then you walked out to the road, where Kirsten picked you up in her car.''

My ex-husband glanced at the gun in my cousin's hand. "You'll never prove it—especially if you plan to accuse our good-old-boy police captain of malfeasance." He looked at me again. And smiled.

If I'd had the gun in my hand, I might have overcome my reluctance to fire it. Gary Gleason had always been infuriatingly confident. I'd have liked to scare the hell out of him, just once.

I looked up at Hal to make sure he appeared sufficiently menacing. He was staring out over the sand flats.

"Headlights," he said.

I followed his gaze. A car was driving slowly through the abandoned housing development.

"Captain Loftus," I presumed. "I called him from Aunt Diana's."

"Jesus Christ!" Gary erupted. "Why'd you do that?"

"I was planning—before I ran into Hal—to lurk around out here until you got tired of waiting for me, and came looking for me. Then I was going to run back to the car and drive off without you. I didn't know what you were planning to do to Sandy—I wanted you out of the way for a while."

Behind me, my cousin said, "Why'd you call in the marines?"

"In case anything went wrong. And if it didn't—well,

I thought it would be a nice irony if Gary had to ride home with Loftus.''

" 'A nice irony?' " My ex-husband scooted farther away from me on the hard sand. "I've got a nice irony for you. Who do you think killed my wife? Who do you think shot your damned detective?''

I watched the captain's car veer toward the sand flats. He'd seen the headlights of the Mercedes.

Gleason looked up at Hal. "I'd get rid of those guns, if I were you.''

Hal stepped back, out of the pool of light.

"You're accusing the captain of murder?'' Gary had always hated the police, a condition doubtless aggravated by being a public defender.

"Kirsten took Bean's gun out of your desk while you were sleeping. She was going to go look for Bean to give the gun back to him. She was going to get him booted out of town because of it, if she could, and you with him. She called me at the hospital to tell me so. That's the last time I ever talked to her. The nurses said she called later, but I was sleeping, and they wouldn't put the call through.''

"So? From this you deduce that Loftus killed her?''

"Who else could it have been? Kirsten called me at around three. Bean was killed a short time later. Right about the time Kirsten would have been driving around near the pier looking for him. I think—'' Gary's eyes were fixed on the car moving cautiously across the flats. "I think she must have ended up witnessing Bean's execution.''

"Execution,'' I repeated. A lot of people would have liked to execute Bean. "Why Loftus?''

"She wasn't killed till after seven. If Bean's killer had recognized Kirsten, or followed the Peugeot, he'd have killed her earlier in the morning. He must have noticed the make and model—that's all. And he didn't get ownership information from Motor Vehicles—not at that hour.

That means he found out from a computer. Only a cop can do that.''

A cop can feed information about a car into a police computer and, within hours, get a printout of local cars of that make, and their owners' addresses. There wouldn't be more than one green Peugeot in a small town like Hillsdale.

I thought of the girl at the car rental concession, telling us that an "older guy," a policeman, had asked who'd rented the black Mustang. I'd assumed that the police routinely checked car rental agencies to learn the names of visiting strangers. But the girl had said the policeman had asked specifically about the black Mustang—which implied he'd seen the Mustang somewhere, then traced ownership to the concession.

I wondered if Sandy had also been down by the pier when Wallace Bean was murdered. If so, it explained several things. It explained Sandy's reluctance to admit he'd arrived in town a day early; it explained why he'd jumped out my window to avoid meeting the police.

"Why Loftus, why *him* in particular?"

"Because he's enough of a goddamned reactionary to think it's his patriotic right to execute someone like Bean. Ever hear him talk about Vietnam? Hansen and Dhzura were heroes to fascists like him." My ex-husband's lips curled disdainfully. "And he's got no inhibitions about taking the law into his own hands, believe me. I know for a fact he ordered his men to beat the crap out of me when we demonstrated to save the wetlands."

The captain pulled up alongside the Mercedes, broadening the band of light on the sand flats. He climbed nimbly out of his black-and-white car, and walked up to us. He wore a thick, hooded jacket. His back was to the light; I couldn't see his face.

"Miss Di Palma? Got your message." His voice was pleasant, curious, even slightly bemused. He pulled a flashlight out of his pocket and shined it slowly over the sand, beyond the area illuminated by the car lights. "Didn't I see someone else out here a minute ago?"

The jacket and the flashlight. Just like the man who'd shot at me from the corridor of Hal's house. "No," I said faintly. "It's just me and Gary."

I stood up, extending my hand to help Gary.

But Captain Loftus moved between us, grasping Gary's arm. He pulled Gary to his feet. He pulled too hard, and Gary staggered forward, tripping over the captain's foot. He fell heavily, the captain's boot catching him in the ribs. Loftus apologized amiably, but I knew the fall had not been accidental.

Jesus, I'd cried in the captain's arms when Sandy was shot. I remembered the warm cologney smell of his shirt, the reassurance of his direct and—I'd thought—kindly manner.

But the hooded jacket, the flashlight, the gratuitous kick in the ribs—I remembered Sandy saying that cops carry thirty-eights; he and Kirsten had both been shot with a thirty-eight.

The wind screamed through the rocks, drowning out the shakiness of my voice. "Gary and I were worried about my cousin, Captain." Gary staggered to his feet, backing away from me and Loftus. "There's no sign of Hal at the house where he's been camping. We wondered if he might have drowned or something."

"No way to find out tonight, I'm afraid, Miss Di Palma. We could have a look at the rocks, I suppose." He motioned for us to follow him, but instead of walking out toward the rocks, he walked back to his car.

He opened the passenger door, and stood there, a dark shape behind the headlights, waiting for us to get in. Gary hugged his ribs, backing cautiously away.

I assumed Loftus meant to drive closer to the jetty.

Whatever he meant to do, I didn't want him to guess anything had changed since I'd phoned him. I got into the car.

The captain drove slowly past Gary without glancing at him. He drove to the very edge of the sand flats, where the tall, sawtooth rocks extended out to the sea. He turned his lights up to high beam.

I thought I saw a shadow at the fringes of the captain's lights. My cousin, moving out of the expanded arc of light.

"Out there," I pointed to a shining triangle of rock up ahead. "Was that someone?"

The high beams lit a surreal landscape of bright, wet surfaces and black shadows, of drifting mist and sheets of spindrift blown off high waves.

Captain Loftus opened his car door and stood, one foot outside the car, his hand still on the steering wheel, looking out over the rocks. And I looked out the passenger window, sure now that I could see movement, that my cousin was out there.

I had the impression he was hurling something.

I heard the captain shout, "Who's there?" as something clattered on the rocks.

The captain pulled a gun out of his holster, hesitated for an instant, then began picking his way over the slick, sharp-edged rocks, using one hand to support himself. In the other he held the gun, held it straight up, ready to aim and fire.

When Loftus was a few hundred feet out onto the rocks, Hal appeared at the passenger door. He flung it open, reached in and cut the lights.

"Get out! Run!"

"But he'll know—"

"Why's he got his gun out? He already knows!" Hal yanked my arm, catching me when I pitched forward onto the sand. "Don't argue! Run!"

I ran. Ran across the sand flats beside Hal, ran as fast as I could toward the Mercedes.

We were about halfway there when the sports car backed up, turned around, and, kicking up a swirl of wet sand, roared toward the main road.

Gary Gleason had stolen my car. For a moment I stood there watching, wishing I'd killed the bastard while I had the chance. And I knew it was my own goddamned fault he'd stranded us there; I'd accused him of Lennart's murder, making it clear I knew all the details. I'd left him little incentive to want me alive.

Hal grabbed my hand. "The houses! Come on!"

Again I ran, watching my beautiful car disappear onto the distant highway. I'd *get* Gleason, goddamn it—if Loftus didn't get me first.

My car raced out of sight, the only landmark in the darkness. We ran and seemed to go nowhere, to be running in a void. I glanced back toward the jetty, my throat aching from gasping damp air. The lights of the police car were sweeping across the sand in a wide circle.

Seconds later, my expensive—and inadequate—shoes hit the concrete of an abandoned street. I could make out the silhouette of sand-wracked houses.

And the police car began rocketing across the flats toward us.

39

"JUST LIKE VIETNAM," Hal observed.

We were in an upstairs bedroom of what had been one of the pricier houses in the development. Hal peered between the boards of a window facing the sand flats. I stood at another window, watching for movement on the black street.

"Who shot you, Hal?"

The wind rattled one of the few remaining panes of glass. Somewhere close, mice scratched at the baseboard.

Finally he said, "There was this girl, Phuyen. The army, in its usual stupid fashion, decided her village was 'inconvenient' because it forced our jeeps to take a short detour through jungle. So they rounded up the Vietnamese and herded them off to this wretched little encampment. Then they went out with tanks to flatten the hootches. But someone kept taking potshots at the soldiers."

"This girl?"

"Well, see," his voice dropped in pitch, "she didn't get rounded up like everyone else. I was going to marry Phuyen. She'd been staying with me; my C.O. was pretty lax about stuff like that. He got the bright idea that I should take her out there with me, to help me find the sniper."

"Did she get shot too, Hal?"

He was silent. I stared into darkness, barely able to make out the houses across the street.

"We were alone together in one of the hootches, the one that belonged to her family. It looked like the sniper had been hiding there; one of her little brothers, probably. Phuyen got this look on her face, I'll never forget it. Like I was part of something disgusting. Like she'd do anything to protect her brothers from me. She grabbed my gun and shot me in the head with it."

It was a few moments before I had the nerve to inquire, "What happened to her, Hal?"

"Summary execution. After being raped a few times. They shot her brothers, too—even the seven-year-old."

I supposed my Aunt Diana had learned the story when the army notified her of Hal's injury. Apparently she'd made a choice. If she mentioned the wound to anyone—even her husband—everyone in town would soon know about it. And everyone would want to know how it had happened. She could lie about it, but Hal—He seemed to delight in thwarting her: leaving his sweet-sixteen present neglected in the driveway; refusing to go by Henry, Junior; turning down Princeton to enroll in junior college like a mill worker's son. No, Hal would tell people the truth: that he'd been intimate with a yellow-skinned girl (they'd whisper that he'd consorted with the enemy); that he'd allowed the tart—one of *them*—to steal an army weapon; and, most shamefully of all, that he'd been shot with his own gun. On the other hand, Hal was maddeningly taciturn. If my aunt said nothing about the injury, Hal would probably not mention it, either. Better to wait and see. If her son was not noticeably disabled, no one would have to know.

"He's coming." Hal's breathing was loud and quick. "He's coming into the house. Squat down behind the dresser. And don't move. Everything creaks in these houses."

I squatted, hearing the crackle of breaking spider webs, skeins of them. I tried to keep still. My hands trembled; I buried them in my pockets. Took shallow breaths. He was coming.

Emmanuel Loftus. (Allow the jury ten seconds to look at his handsome, wise, kindly face.) Lost a beloved son in the war. Lived with that loss day in and day out for fourteen years—as perhaps some of you have done. Believed with painful, passionate intensity that the war could have been won—that his son and thousands of other sons, *your* sons, could have been spared. Not by cowardly retreat. That's not what we are about, as a nation. But by victory.

Emmanuel Loftus was not the only American who believed in victory. Two men in particular embodied the spirit, the patriotism, the idealism that might have won a war, might have freed a people. Might have kept alive an American dream. I refer of course to Senator Harley Hansen and Senator Garth Dzhura. (Ten seconds.) As you are probably aware, a man called Wallace Bean set out one day to destroy not just these two duly-elected representatives—but to destroy the very America they symbolized. The America that loves freedom enough to sacrifice—to fight, *really fight*—for it.

Emmanuel Loftus was a good father. A patriot. An officer of justice. And as a father, as a patriot, as an officer of justice, it offended him, it insulted him, it sickened him, that a man could murder an American ideal (five second pause), and be free to walk the streets a scant year later! It offended him and insulted him and sickened him that a man could widow two women and orphan seven children—with impunity!—because he *watched too much television*!

"Hal," I whispered, "do you believe in poetic justice?"

"I don't believe in any kind of justice."

I heard a thump downstairs.

Jesus God, Loftus had no right! No right to spill Bean's blood or anybody's else's!

And what about Bean? What about *me*—justifying, apologizing, making excuses for the senators' murder?

Cautious footsteps below. I glanced at my cousin; he was a shape within a shadow. It wasn't fair—Loftus was *my* penance, not his.

When the footsteps moved toward the staircase, I disregarded Hal's warning and tiptoed across the room to where he crouched behind an abandoned desk. I wanted to be near him.

Almost immediately the door began to open; I could hear the rasp of rusty hinges. Light filtered through dust motes; Loftus's flashlight was trained on the hallway floor.

I focused so completely on the light, on the sounds Loftus made, that I didn't hear the sounds outside until the captain grumbled, ''Christ A'mighty, what now?'' The light went off. He clomped over to the window I had recently used as a lookout post.

Loftus stood where I'd stood, looking through gaps in the slats.

I heard the sound of wheels bumping over potholes, not directly below, but close by, at the fringes of the abandoned development. Somewhere a door slid open, with a thump that echoed through the empty streets. It was a van, the Oregon news van, I was sure. I'd asked my Uncle Henry to go outside at 11:45 and send that vanful of reporters to the jetty.

I'd wanted additional insurance, in case my disappearing trick did not work out, in case I wasn't able to slip away from Gary Gleason. And in case Captain Loftus did not get my message in time.

I felt a prickle of relief. Perhaps Loftus would leave the house now, would go outside to send the reporters away.

I could hear him step away from the window, muttering

under his breath. Then he stopped. Five feet from where Hal and I huddled behind the desk.

I wasn't sure at first that Loftus had seen us. I wasn't sure until I heard the sound. It was just a quiet click in the dark, but I recognized it. He'd pulled back the hammer of his gun.

Apparently, Hal heard the sound, too. He hurled himself against me, knocking me facedown on the rough wood floor. Grit scraped my lips and filled my nostrils. My wrist bent under the shifting weight of our bodies, and I heard myself cry out. I could smell my cousin's fear. Maybe it was my own.

I arched my back and twisted; caught Hal off balance and pushed him off me. Scrambled away on all fours. Loftus would shoot me first; maybe Hal could get away.

"They're reporters!" I panted. "They're here because I told Sandy Arkelett we were coming here!" I talked because I'm trained to talk. Couldn't seem to catch my breath. All I could see of Loftus was a darker shade of black against the boarded-up window. "I got you out here so Sandy could hold a press conference at the hospital!" A midnight press conference? I stifled a surge of panic. "The reporters knew you shot Sandy, and they know why. So it's no use killing us because they won't believe—"

The captain's voice was surprisingly genial. "Two suspects fled when I ordered them to halt. I gave chase, gave warning, then shot. I didn't know who they were. A great tragedy."

Loftus was standing over me now; still just a dark shape. I tried to distinguish his gun; couldn't remember whether he carried it in his left or right hand. Stared without blinking until spots of light danced in front of my eyes.

"Gary Gleason will tell them you knew it was me!" I sounded breathless; sounded trapped in a lie. I forced myself to close my eyes. To visualize a jury. I felt my throat relax, my chest expand.

Loftus was saying, "You were dragged into an empty house by an unknown suspect. He pulled you in front of him when I shot. A great tragedy." Warmed by his Oklahoma accent, the phrase rang with sincerity. "I shot the suspect afterward, of course."

"Your 'suspect' is the mayor's son!" I made myself pause. Four beats: enough time to fear, not enough time to ponder. "Besides, Sandy's already told the reporters you shot him. They'll check the bullets against your gun."

There was a slight catch in the captain's breathing. "Your out-of-town newsmen, they've all gone home by now." He seemed to be reassuring himself. "And the locals, they know me. They won't believe some slick P.I. from the big city. Specially when I arrest him for murdering Kirsten Strindberg." He added thoughtfully, "Guess I better get myself a new thirty-eight, though."

"They'll check the serial number against the one listed for your gun in the police records."

"It's not hard to change police records." His voice regained confidence. "I've done it before."

There's a moment, in almost every trial, when a lawyer's best arguments are disregarded, or even ridiculed, by the judge; when the judge says, "Well, if that's all you have to say about it . . ." In that moment, as short as a comma in a sentence whose conclusion you don't want to hear, a litigator will say any goddamned thing that comes to mind.

I said, "Sander Arkelett is FBI."

His tone was skeptical. "Not the FBI's jurisdiction." He was right—but he wasn't shooting. There had to be some paranoia there. Maybe enough to exploit.

"Continued surveillance of Wallace Bean, until it could be determined whether he posed a threat to other federal officials."

Loftus stood motionless in the dark room, apparently

thinking about it. He finally said, "FBI always checks in with us."

"You shot Bean before Sandy had a chance to check in."

"So why didn't Arkelett arrest me?"

He was beginning to believe me. My voice had to be just right; he would hear the tone, not the words. "Sandy was investigating possible collaboration by other officers."

Loftus didn't respond. He stepped cautiously backward, toward the window. I could hear voices outside, but not close enough.

"Let us go, Captain. Your luck ran out when you didn't kill Sander. He's told all those reporters outside that he saw you murder Bean, and that he saw you go to Kirsten's house later that morning. He's an eyewitness, and a federal agent to boot. It's no use killing anyone else now."

I could hear Hal's ragged breathing, the scrape of the captain's shoe over bits of debris. For a few minutes—maybe only seconds—Loftus kept us in a limbo of silence.

Then he lunged at me.

Gun metal banged my cheek, a steel-trap grip wrenched my shoulder. I lurched forward, my fingers sliding through a slimy substance on the floor. And Loftus's arm caught me around the neck. His damp sleeve filled my mouth as he yanked me to my feet. Pain shot down my spine.

I heard Hal scramble toward us.

I stopped him with the warning, "The gun's at my throat!"

The captain's thirty-eight was buried painfully beneath my jaw. It reeked of lubricating oil. My arm was twisted behind me, my hand bent backward nearly to the snapping point. Loftus breathed over my shoulder; I could feel his wet jacket on my neck, could smell cinnamon gum on his breath. His voice was quiet and determined. "You, boy. Go ahead of us where I can see you, and keep your hands up. We'll just go on downstairs and see what the reporters have to say.'' He jerked my arm upward and back, sending a searing jolt all the way to my pectorals. "And I'll do the talking, please, Miss Di Palma."

40

THE NEWS VAN was parked at the edge of the development, where the sand flats began. I couldn't see anyone near it. I could just make out the white of the van and the contrasting darkness of its open door.

A hundred feet beyond it, flashlights bobbed over the flats. Three figures were silhouetted behind the lights, walking through blowing sand toward the rock jetty. The reporters had apparently taken my Uncle Henry at his word when he'd relayed my message to meet me "out on the jetty."

"Hullo!" Loftus called. The echo of waves crashing on the rocks drowned out his shout. Loftus tried again without success.

The wind sucked my hair back, slicing through my coat, pelting my legs with clumps of damp sand and shards of brittle dune grass. I stood very still; my arm was a hair's breadth from dislocation and Loftus's gun was aimed at the back of my cousin's head. I watched the reporters' flashlights sweep the sand, moving closer to the jetty.

I had discovered in Loftus a well of guilty paranoia; and

because of it, he'd been chary of dismissing my lie. But the minute those reporters denied my story—

A dark shape skirted the white of the van. Damn! Someone had remained behind with the equipment.

An FBI agent would never call a news conference *before* he'd made an arrest—he might as well buy his suspect an airplane ticket to Brazil. After two murders and one attempt, trepidation had made Loftus gullible—but it wouldn't take much to restore his confidence. Just a word or two from this reporter.

And it wouldn't take Loftus long to invoke his police authority and send all four reporters away.

Hal stood about eighteen inches in front of me and the captain, his fingers laced on top of his head. The reporter at the news van would certainly notice it. He'd remember it when the captain claimed his "suspect" had tried to escape, pulling me into the line of fire. The reporter would also remember that I'd stood by while the captain kept his gun aimed at my cousin. He'd conclude—and report—that I'd approved of Hal's arrest. There would be an inquiry, of course. Hal was the mayor's son, after all; and I was a public figure, of sorts.

But the world would learn about Hal's injury—how it had happened, the aftermath of brain damage, his refusal to take antipsychotic drugs, his transient lifestyle. Psychiatrists would appear on *A.M. San Francisco* to confirm that my cousin's psychological profile was consistent with a homicide spree. The captain would be praised for having arrested Hal, in spite of having been forced to kill him. And as for me—everyone would agree my death was "a great tragedy."

I inhaled a bracing lungful of ocean wind. If I could somehow cue the reporter—But I realized Loftus would order the van away and frog-march me away, Hal two paces ahead, if I so much as sneezed.

The captain called out to the figure beside the van. "Police officer! Step forward."

The reporter ducked sideways, as if contemplating flight.

"Police!" Loftus shouted with greater authority. "Step forward!"

The figure hesitated, then came slowly closer. He was a very tall man of average build. I couldn't see his face.

Loftus barked, "Have you been talking to a man named Arkelett?"

Even in the dark, the figure radiated reluctance.

Loftus crushed my wrist in exasperation. "Answer my question!"

"Sander Arkelett?" came the choked response. "Yes, sir."

I'd have recognized that faintly accented voice anywhere. It was the boy I'd known as Dieter Strindberg. The boy who'd fled from me a few hours earlier. Apparently he *had* taken shelter in this forsaken bit of suburbia. He'd probably approached the news van to request a ride home.

And now his "Yes, sir," was buying me an extra minute of life. I took a deep breath: As a child, I'd loved wild, windy nights. Hillsdale had seemed a good enough place to me, then.

One more question, and Loftus would know the truth. I wondered about reincarnation, realizing sadly that It—or They—would never let me be a litigator again.

"Did he say anything about who killed Wallace Bean?" Loftus's words swept through the deserted streets, echoing *Bean, Bean*.

I waited. The jury was in.

The boy answered, "Yes."

I believed, at first, that I'd heard what I wished to hear. An aural mirage.

"What did Arkelett say?" Loftus's voice lost all pretense of confidence.

"He said—" The boy broke off, apparently frightened of the man interrogating him in the darkness. He looked over his shoulder.

Several hundred feet behind the van, two of the three flashlights began bobbing back toward us.

"Tell me, goddamn it!" Desperation crackled in the command.

The boy turned back to Loftus, hugging himself, hunching his shoulders. "He said it was the captain of the police. That he must be careful because—"

The boy didn't finish his sentence. Captain Loftus moaned, "Madonna in heaven!" and released my arm.

I felt a tide of relief from my fingertips to my shoulder. I watched Hal lower his hands and turn his head.

And I realized what the boy had said. He'd said the one, the only thing that could make Loftus believe it was all true—my whole preposterous story. I glanced over my shoulder.

A flash of blue and orange flame exploded right behind me. The air-shattering blast sent me staggering. I clapped my hands over my ears as the echo of it boomed through the empty streets. I coughed out acrid smoke, blinking a sulfurous sting from my eyes.

In front of me, my cousin doubled over.

I watched him drop, vaguely aware of someone screaming German phrases.

And I dropped too, bruising my knees on the ruined concrete. My cousin had been shot. Shot. Because I'd involved him in my stupid scheme.

"Hal!" The wind whisked his name away; I felt rather than heard myself speak it.

I touched my cousin's back. And to my great relief, he moved. He pushed me aside, crawling over my legs to get to the captain.

Then Hal stopped, still on all fours, still straddling my legs. He stopped cold. Panting. Watching.

I twisted beneath him, frightened to numbness, expecting to see the dark outline of a gun pointed at his head.

Loftus was on his knees. He still held the thirty-eight, but his arm was down. The gun barrel scraped the concrete. Even in the darkness, I could see that his head was bowed, that he swayed slightly. He's praying, I thought bitterly. Please, God, don't acquit him.

And then Loftus folded over and tumbled sideways.

A ray of light jerked over the uneven street, bouncing over the captain's hooded head, momentarily spotlighting his hand, the fingers still gripping the gun.

I heard pounding, felt it reverberate through the concrete. Running footsteps. I looked behind me. Light dazzled my eyes.

Hal crawled over me, putting his body between me and Loftus.

The reporters reached us, their voices breathless, high-pitched with excitement. "Was that a *shot*? Where's Di Palma? Are you guys okay?"

Then both flashlights discovered the captain. Stopped. Moved closer.

In the cast-back glow of light, I saw the fat reporter with the clipped beard. His hair fell over his forehead in stringy dishevelment, his beard glistened damply. He stared down, mouth gaping.

Behind him, the other newsman murmured, "Right in the eyeball! Kee-rist!"

The fat reporter blinked at his companion for a moment. Then he gestured toward the van. "You'd better start setting up the lights."

41

IT WAS A rough night, an uphill battle making the captain's underlings believe he'd killed himself or anybody else. I sported a few new bruises, from being tossed against a wall by a cop with a clamped jaw and tears of anger in his eyes. I was strip-searched for no good reason, and though I repeatedly requested some, no coffee ever found its way into the interrogation room.

But it was over by late morning. Hal and the German boy corroborated my story. It was also consistent with what the Oregon reporters had discovered. But the clincher was the physical evidence. A bullet fired from the captain's standard-issue thirty-eight matched the bullets taken out of Kirsten Strindberg and Sander Arkelett. And out of Loftus's own skull.

As I left the building, one of the cops who'd searched my house stopped me at the door.

"I'm Terry Dickens. You don't remember me, do you? We were in Algebra Two together."

I did remember him, after a moment. I'd thought he looked familiar, when he came to search my house.

He said, "I guess the fellas gave you a lot of shit, huh?"

"I guess so."

"We all liked the captain." He stepped closer. His skin was oily, spotted with tiny black grains, just as it had been in high school. "But between us, I wasn't all that surprised. I used to be good buds with John, the captain's son. There was a lot of bad feelings on John's part when the captain made him enlist."

I considered telling Terry Dickens that the captain needn't have forced John Loftus into the army; that John hadn't screwed up the exhaust system of my car, after all. But it was a long story, and I was heartily sick of men in blue uniforms.

Terry Dickens continued, "When John got killed, the captain he got like superpatriotic, you know, like he had to think it was worth it, sending John over there. If Wallace Bean had asked me, boy, I'd have told him, stay the hell away from Hillsdale. 'Cause the captain was a big fan of those two senators, and he didn't think much of you getting Bean off like that."

"*I* didn't get Bean off," I explained mechanically. "A jury acquitted him."

"Now that I think of it," Dickens rubbed a bit of the shine off his nose, "Captain had me and another uniform go out to Old Town and check IDs, you know, generally hassle the winos, the night Bean got offed. I wonder if he *wanted* us to find Bean. You know, and eliminate the temptation."

"Could you give me a ride somewhere?"

Dickens smuggled me out of the building through the downstairs garage (reporters outside, he explained). At my request, he drove me to County Hospital.

I repeated our conversation to Sander Arkelett.

Sandy looked terrible, pale and full of tubes, but the doctors said there was no sign of infection.

He said, in a wheezy whisper, "Scared hell out of me, Laura. I flew in a night early and there was Wallace Bean on the plane. I rented a car and offered him a lift. Took him to a flophouse near the canneries. So I'm still slouching around three or four hours later keeping an eye on him, when I see this plainclothes cop get out of an unmarked car.'' He smiled slightly, wincing as the tube taped to his upper lip shifted. ''I can always spot an unmarked. And the way a cop walks. Anyway, Bean and the cop got to talking, and next thing I know the cop's handing Bean a revolver.''

I sighed. ''Loftus must have had the same idea that Kirsten got, later. He must have spotted Bean around town, and decided to set him up for a bust by giving him an unregistered gun. Then he arranged for a couple of cops to go into the neighborhood and shake down strangers. But by then, Bean had left Old Town. He'd come to my house. The cops didn't bust anybody, so Loftus was forced to go look for Bean again. When he finally found him near the Lucky Logger, Bean didn't have the gun anymore. Maybe Loftus tried to get Bean to take the matching gun, but by then I'd warned Wally to be careful. And I guess maybe the whole thing got to Loftus. Here's a sleazy, volatile killer out on the streets after only eleven months—I guess Loftus must have decided to skip the half-measures and shoot him. Execute him for crimes committed.''

''Probably right,'' Sandy rasped. ''I followed Bean to your house. Saw him go in with the gun, and leave without it—I knew you'd take the damn thing away from him. I followed him back down to the pier, and here comes Plainclothes again, with what looks like the same damn gun.'' The wheezing grew worse.

''It's okay, Sandy. Don't talk. I know what happened.''

Loftus shot Bean, looked around, and saw a car taking off down the street. Kirsten Strindberg. She'd driven to the pier because she knew Bean had been lurking there. She'd heard him tell me so, when he came to my house. Kirsten suspected I was in town to make trouble for her, so she'd decided to make a little trouble for me. She'd taken the gun out of my drawer while I was passed out on the couch, and she'd gone to give it back to Bean. Maybe she assumed Bean would do something stupid, like shoot it off; or maybe she intended to find a cop and have him busted for weapons possession. But she ended up seeing him get murdered instead. "Kirsten saw Loftus execute Bean. And Loftus saw Kirsten's green Peugeot."

Sandy nodded weakly, closing his eyes. When his breathing was less labored, he said, "I'd cased Gleason's place last time I was in town, so I knew who the Peugeot belonged to. I got to Gleason's in time to see Strindberg cross the street and stick the gun under the driver's seat of your Mercedes. Not like you to leave the car door unlocked, Laura."

"Hal drove me home. He got out on that side. I didn't think to check."

"Strindberg looked nervous enough to fall to pieces."

"Stupid woman." My antipathy had survived her. "Ironic, isn't it, Sandy? She gets rid of *that* gun, only to have Loftus plant its twin in her house. He must have been irritated as hell when the twenty-two wouldn't fire again, and he had to use his own police revolver to kill Kirsten. I guess he left the twenty-two there to connect her with Bean's murder and add a little confusion to a case he didn't want solved."

"Well, I didn't care for all this coming and going of guns. I spent the night in my car, down the street from your house, keeping an eye on it for you. And what do I do but nod out for a while. I open my eyes and Plainclothes is coming out of Strindberg's house. He starts looking up and down the street and I slide out of the car real fast, keeping low. I'm in your bushes by the time he walks over and starts looking the Mustang over. I guess he remembered seeing it parked down by the cannery earlier. So he leaves, and I've got this problem. Who the hell's going to believe the captain of police shot anybody? He denies it, and where does that leave me? Out of town on a rail, and maybe facing a hearing to revoke my P.I.

license, if Loftus is feeling mean. I need evidence. More than just my word against his.''

"Loftus must have run a license-plate check on the Mustang. It took him to the car rental place at the airport, where the girl—who has quite a crush on you, by the way, Sandy—gave Loftus your name. So he had your name, but no idea who you were or what you looked like. Not until one of his officers stopped my car to take me to police headquarters the other day. Remember, Sandy, before Hal and I got into the police car, I told you to meet me at Hal's house? I called you by name. The cop must have repeated the conversation to Loftus. It was Loftus who fired those shots at me. He knew which house Hal had been staying in; the cops had been keeping an eye on it to make sure Hal didn't start any fires. He went out there to get rid of you, Sandy, in case you'd seen anything. He'd probably have shot Hal by mistake if I hadn't shouted out his name. But I suppose he missed me on purpose. He didn't have any reason to kill me. Just scare me. Anyway,'' I concluded, "I guess it's no mystery why you climbed out my window and ran away when the police came to my house.''

Sandy smiled, with his eyelids more than his lips.

"And also why you left my aunt's party.''

"I didn't want you introducing me to Loftus. I'd parked my car far enough away that I didn't worry about him spotting it. But I thought I'd better hang around outside and make sure you got home okay. So ten minutes later, out comes Loftus and searches your car.''

"Then it was Loftus who moved the revolver,'' I realized. "He found Bean's gun—*his* gun—under my seat where Kirsten had put it. I wonder why he took it out?''

"Well, honey, every word you say gets picked up by the wire services. Maybe he thought it would be safer to leave you clean out of the whole mess, if he could.''

"Maybe,'' I conceded. Loftus had been unvaryingly

polite to me. And surprisingly uninquisitive, every time he'd questioned me. "But why did he put it back?"

"He'd shot me by then. He might be needing a scapegoat. And you were my—" He looked away. "He might need to build a case against you, if push came to shove."

"He came to talk to me in the hospital, and I challenged him. I acted suspicious that he hadn't questioned me more aggressively."

"Bad mistake, Laura. That's probably when he decided to put the gun back."

"Speaking of mistakes, why'd you go into the bushes, Sandy?"

"After Loftus searched your car, he took off in his unmarked. I thought he was gone for good. But I guess he'd spotted me lurking around. He must have parked his car and doubled back." Sandy's face looked pinched. He obviously didn't relish recounting this part of his story. "You left the party, and I wanted to follow you home. I thought I'd be extra cautious. Get to my car through the gully, in case Loftus was still in the neighborhood. Well—Turned out Loftus was coming across the gully, right toward me. I realized it about a quarter of the way across. I doubled back. Almost made it to your aunt's yard before he caught up."

I stared out the window I'd made the nurses lock in Gary Gleason's presence. Sandy himself had taken the wisest precaution. He'd told the cops it had been too dark to see his attacker. He knew he'd be a sitting duck for Loftus, otherwise.

"Why didn't you tell me about the German boy, whatever his name is?"

"It's Dieter Strindberg. That much is true. In fact, it's all true, almost. It's just . . . I didn't know you all that well when I first told you about him. And back then I had the impression you hated Kirsten Strindberg about as much as you could hate anyone. I didn't know how you'd feel about helping her nephew, her dead brother's only kid. So I told you the kid was Lennart's brother.''

"Why didn't you tell me you were working for him?"

Sandy's eyelids drooped, but he looked more sick than sleepy. "I never do tell anyone who my clients are, honey. I'm not supposed to. That's the private part of private investigation."

"There's something else you didn't tell me."

Sandy looked up at me, volunteering nothing.

"You stole Kirsten's will, didn't you, Sandy? You left that out of your sequence of events, but it's true, isn't it? After Loftus came out of Kirsten's house, you went in and found her dead. Most people keep a copy of their will at home—you know that. So you snooped around until you found it. You stole Kirsten's will.''

"What makes you think she even made a will? All you've got is Gleason's word for it. And he's a lawyer— wouldn't he keep another copy somewhere?''

"At his office. You stole that copy, too. You must have done it while Gary was still in the hospital, the morning after Kirsten was killed. Before I picked you up at the airport.''

Sandy closed his eyes.

"Gary must have been frantic when he realized both copies were gone—and he undoubtedly told the cops about it. So when they found my fingerprints on Kirsten's letter drawer—and they must have found *some*—Loftus was pretty much obligated to go after a search warrant. It would have looked odd if he hadn't. But *I* didn't take that will. And *Loftus* had no reason to take it. When it comes right down to it, the only person who *did* have a reason was Dieter Strindberg—and you were working for him.''

I looked at Sandy's arms, where tubes stabbed the bruised skin of his inner elbows. I looked at the smaller tube snaking into his nose. His eyes were sunken, ringed with gray. He didn't need this.

"You destroyed Kirsten's will so Gary Gleason wouldn't inherit all of Kirsten's separate property—like that financial district building. If I remember the rules of intestate succession, Kirsten's brother—or in this case his surviving child—will get half. Your client will get half."

"If it was up to me, Dieter would get the whole damn thing!" Sandy opened his eyes. A spark of anger lent his ashen face vitality. "Gleason murdered Lennart Strindberg, but we'll never prove it, Laura! That's the goddamned system for you!"

I nodded. A little rough justice had been effected; who the hell was I to complain?

42

I FOUND MY Mercedes parked in front of my house. My bastard of an ex-husband had returned it after stranding me on the sand flats.

And I found my Uncle Henry in my living room, stockinged feet on the coffee table as he sipped whiskey and read what looked like a budget report.

"Don't get up." I bent to pick up an envelope on the floor beneath the mail slot.

It was a telegram from Doron White himself, senior partner of White, Sayres & Speck. It read, *Our regrets re Wallace Bean. Congratulations on ascertaining his assassin. Assume Arkelett there at your behest on Bean-related*

matter. Insurer to underwrite hospital expenses and ar-
range helicopter transport to S.F. General. Urge you to
cut short leave of absence. So-called law school murderer
wishes to retain your services immediately.

I looked up to find my uncle standing solicitously beside
me. "Not bad news, is it, Laura?"

I shook my head. "No, good news. I'm going back to
San Francisco as soon as I can get packed. I've got a big
case. Probably the hottest case in the state."

My uncle looked around the well-built old Victorian.
"Don't you have a lease?"

"I'll buy out of it."

He put his arm around me. I could smell whiskey and
after-shave, see the sparkle in his dark eyes. "I'll tell you
what, Laura, why don't I just stay on here for the time
being? Sublease the place from you?"

My Aunt Diana would love that. "Great. Let Papa have
one of the rooms, will you?"

My uncle smiled wryly. "He's already asked."

I climbed the stairs and crawled into the bath. I was
dressing when I heard a tap at my bedroom door.

"It's me. Hal."

My stomach knotted, then fluttered. The way it does
before closing arguments.

I opened the door.

For a moment, we just looked at one another. Hal's face
was bruised, his lip split. He was unshaven, his hair damp
from the foggy walk from the police station.

But he looked younger than he had a few days earlier.
His face looked serious, but not bitter. There were lines
around his eyes, but his unconscious wince was gone.

I touched the bruise on his forehead. "You can't say
I'm a dull person to be around."

"I'd never say that," he agreed.

"I'm going back to the city, Hal. I've got the kind of
case criminal lawyers drool over. Multiple murders, lots

of publicity. Really interesting stuff—not just a panicked shot in a liquor store.''

"I see.''

"I mean, I know no one else has the right to kill another person! But—"

"Murderers are entitled to the best defense. Isn't that how the cliché goes?''

"No, I won't pretend it's altruism. I love criminal law, Hal. And I'm very good at it.'' So why did I sound defensive?

"Still worried about poetic justice, cousin?''

"Yes,'' I admitted reluctantly. "I guess so. Karma. Whatever you want to call it.''

"A major occupational hazard—for everyone.'' He smiled. "But the kind of week you've had, I'd say it's a wash. You might even be a little ahead of the game.''

"I don't suppose you'd come to San Francisco with me?'' Framing a question in the negative; I knew better than that. "You wouldn't have to put up with me that much. I'm an awful workaholic; seventy, eighty hours a week.''

"And I'll bet you *talk* about your job the rest of the time.''

"I probably do.'' An admission against interest; I was blowing my case. I stepped closer, resting my hands on his chest. "San Francisco's the greatest town in the world, Hal. You could wander around every day and never get tired of it. You could learn the bus routes; you could get anywhere without driving.'' I heard desperation creep into my voice. "If you wanted to travel, I'd understand. I'd go with you as often as I could. I make such a lot of money, Hal. You'd be shocked how much. I could send you anywhere. And I could buy you music, and tapes of people reading books. And a television. I could buy a big fancy one, with a video recorder so you could rent movies.''

The more I talked, the more I seemed to be insulting him. I'd have to do better than this for my new client.

"I don't need a lot of money. And I need a big TV about as much as Wallace Bean did."

"Sure—you've proved you can do without stuff. But I'm not offering you what your father offered you. I don't want to *help* you."

"But that would be the effect of the arrangement, wouldn't it?" His tone was neutral.

"Anything wrong with that?"

"I should go with the smart money. That what you're saying?"

"You could think of it as easy. Easy money."

"No. I don't think we'd have a very easy time together, Laura. But—" He frowned down at me. "If I say no, you might start plotting against me, like you did with Gleason. And hell, I've seen you talk a cop right into his grave."

"Don't risk it, Hal."

"Handicapped old vet like me." He shook his head. "I'd better not."

ABOUT THE AUTHOR

Lia Matera is a graduate of Hastings College of Law, where she was editor of the *Constitutional Law Review*. She was later a teaching fellow at Stanford Law School. Since 1987 she has been a critically acclaimed mystery writer. *Where Lawyers Fear To Tread* was her debut—and also the launch for one of her series heroines: Willa Jansson. The novel was nominated for an Anthony Award, and its sequel—*A Radical Departure*—was nominated for both an Anthony and an Edgar Allan Poe Award. Subsequent novels include *The Smart Money* (the debut of Laura Di Palma), *Hidden Agenda*, *The Good Fight*, and *Prior Convictions*. Ms. Matera lives in Santa Cruz, California, with her son.